Horace Horrise throws a party, or Horace Horrise and Charlie, or Ho
Horace Horrise and his second-hand activity trousers, or Horace H
Horrise gets grounded for a week, or Horace Horrise and The Grar
locked gate, or Horace Horrise and the blue rope, or Horace Horri
way to the scout hut, or Horace Horrise and the kangaroos, or Hor
Horace Horrise is not left on his own, or Horace Horrise and the a
Horace Horrise makes some new friends, or Horace Horrise gets in
Chislehurst, or Horace Horrise and The Lion's Head, or Horace Horrise the lion tamer, or Horace Horrise and
the kangaroo, or Horace Horrise rides in Eric's pouch, or Daddy kangaroos don't have pouches, or Horace Horrise
gets shortened, or Horace Horrise eats kangaroo at The Lion's Head, or Horace Horrise and the bouncing
kangaroos, or Kangaroos don't have wings, or Horace Horrise and his smart scout leader, or Horace Horrise the
timekeeper, or Horace Horrise is Badhorace, or Horace Horrise and 3rd Chislehurst Scout Group, or Horace Horrise
with soap and water, or Horace Horrise and no diversions, or Horace Horrise and the kangaroo patrols, or Horace
Horrise sticks with the birds, or Horace Horrise the chief fundraiser, or Horace Horrise the Raven, or Horace Horrise
the Ravings, or Horace Horrise meets Edward, Melanie and Archie, or Horace Horrise meets the Peckers, or
Horace Horrise and his favourite things, or Horace Horrise goes red and the scouts fall silent, or Raving Horace
Horrise arrives, or Horace Horrise and his anxious mother, or Charlie brings Horace Horrise home, or Horace
Horrise and the slice of Victoria sponge, or Horace Horrise doesn't need bribing, or Horace Horrise demolished the
cake, or Horace Horrise is getting invested, or Horace Horrise gets back in one piece, or Horace Horrise and the
smallholder badge, or Horace Horrise grants his mother's wish, or Horace Horrise and the secret potatoes, or
Horace Horrise and the broken mirror confession, or Horace Horrise for one night only, or Horace Horrise and the
fiftieth birthday celebrations, or Horace Horrise and the churchyard, or Horace Horrise and the Scout Promise, or
Horace Horrise and squash, buns and cake, or Horace Horrise and the daffodil bulbs, or Horace Horrise digs up a
body, or Horace Horrise and the escaping bodies, or Horace Horrise and the worms, or Horace Horrise and Arnold
John Grieve, or Horace Horrise doesn't get in first, or Horace Horrise and the first fairy cake, or Horace Horrise and
the graves of the famous and infamous, or Horace Horrise and a Member of Parliament, a poet and a world record
breaker, or Horace Horrise and any questions, or Horace Horrise and knock, knock, knock, or Horace Horrise and
the mourners, or Horace Horrise and manual work, or Horace Horrise helps the church people, or Horace Horrise
and his worm diet, or Horace Horrise and the potatoes and pumpkin, or Horace Horrise and the trap, or Horace
Horrise plays it safe, or Horace Horrise looks for Vera, or Horace Horrise and the bean spiller, or Horace Horrise
and the feminist, or Horace Horrise and the smart summer dress, or Horace Horrise and Edward's pressing
question, or Horace Horrise and his frenzied imagination, or Horace Horrise and the community projects, or Horace
Horrise with the old men and their plots, or Horace Horrise and the lazy men, or Horace Horrise and the bindweed,
or Horace Horrise and the turd trailer, or Horace Horrise and the horse manure, or Horace Horrise and the kangaroo
talk, or Horace Horrise and the manure spreaders, or Horace Horrise and the black sacks, or Horace Horrise and
the mole invasion, or Horace Horrise and the two doughnuts, or Horace Horrise and the spoilsports, or Horace
Horrise and the triple chocolate doughnut, or Horace Horrise and the farming and livestock, or Horace Horrise and
the cats, dogs and rabbits, or Horace Horrise bee hives, or Horace Horrise is offended, or Horace Horrise works like
a Trojan, or Horace Horrise and the Rhode Island Red, or Horace Horrise and Albert the cockerel, or Horace Horrise
and the honeycomb and honey, or Horace Horrise and the small matter, or Horace Horrise and his disappearing
brother, or Horace Horrise and the chips and ice cream, or Horace Horrise and the garden lawn, or Horace Horrise
and two hundred turves, or Horace Horrise and the memorial garden, or Horace Horrise and the Champagne, or
Horace Horrise and the quick sandwich, or Horace Horrise and the out of tune adults, or Horace Horrise and the
bamboo sticks, or Horace Horrise and the garden machinery, or Horace Horrise and the rotavators, or Horace
Horrise and the hermit crab, or Horace Horrise and the runner beans, or Horace Horrise and the broken glasses, or
Horace Horrise and the cup and ball game, or Horace Horrise and the six roosters, or Horace Horrise and the
periscope, or Horace Horrise and the transformational gardening, or Horace Horrise and the beer barrel, or Horace
Horrise and his brother's cooking, or Horace Horrise and the early breakfast, or Horace Horrise and Zen, or Horace
Horrise and the huge hammer, or Horace Horrise and Chislehurst Marquees, or Horace Horrise meets Billy and
Webbo, or Horace Horrise and Mammoth, or Horace Horrise and the molten mud, or Horace Horrise and the milky
sangria, or Horace Horrise and the camomile and spiced apple with cinnamon, or Horace Horrise and the four
teaspoonfuls, or Horace Horrise and the generous donation, or Horace Horrise and the churchwarden, or Horace
Horrise and the peach schnapps, or Horace Horrise and the laundry basket, or Horace Horrise and the hose, or
Horace Horrise and the rocket, or Horace Horrise and Chislehurst Catering, or Horace Horrise and Chislehurst
String Quartet, or Horace Horrise and Old Elthamian's mud bath, or Horace Horrise goes as white as a sheet, or
Horace Horrise and Edgar Fripp, or Horace Horrise writes a letter, or Horace Horrise and Chesney Golf Club, or
Horace Horrise and the happy birthday, or Horace Horrise and Bert's Sloe Gin, or Horace Horrise and the four black
bags, or Horace Horrise and Great Uncle Stanley, or Horace Horrise and the bondaged geriatric punk, or Horace
Horrise and Auntie May, or Horace Horrise and the wedding cake, or Horace Horrise and the grass seed, or Horace
Horrise and the car park in his road, or Horace Horrise and the Organising Abilities activity badge, or Horace Horrise
gets prepared, or Horace Horrise gets nearer to being invested, or Horace Horrise comes up smelling of roses once
again.

John Hemming-Clark

© Searchline Publishing 2017
First edition 2017

ISBN: 978 1 897864 37 1

British Library Cataloguing in Publication Data available
Published by Searchline Publishing, Searchline House,
Holbrook Lane, Chislehurst, Kent, BR7 6PE, UK

Tel: 020 8468 7945
www.inyougo.webeden.co.uk

Printed in England by: www.catfordprint.co.uk

For Bubbs and Pike. Two fantastic young scouters who appear
in these adventures more often than they realise.

The stories that appear in The Adventures of Horace Horrise
have been inspired, not only by Bubbs and Pike, but also by
numerous scout leaders in Chislehurst, Bromley District and
further afield, not forgetting the Guides that we meet at
international jamborees and other events from time to time,
who don't have nicknames and so wouldn't be quite so
anonymous. Without these leaders who are such generous
providers, for free, of their time these books would not be
possible. Scouting is fun! If you're interested in joining,
whatever your age, go to www.scouts.org.uk and type in your
postcode. If you type in "Chislehurst" you might even find me!

Introduction
Ideally, my friends, you will already have read books one and two but if not, or if you've forgotten, the protagonists are:

The Horrise Family
David Horrise: Father
Karen Horrise: Mother
Sam Horrise: 14/15-year-old son
Horace Horrise: 11-year-old-son
Olivia Horrise: 8-year-old daughter

Friends and Neighbours
Charlie: Horace's best friend, scout
Tanya: Sam's girlfriend
Skip / John: Scout Leader
Archie: Scout, Patrol Leader
Susie: The Horrises' next-door neighbour

Horace has been accepted into scouts but has yet to get to a meeting and so, in book three in The Adventures of Horace Horrise series, Charlie has to take him just to make sure he arrives. But that's just the start of this particular adventure.

Thinking up a snappy title for each book is often something of a challenge and so, for book three, I had a bit of a meltdown and then just strung all the possibilities together. Having done so I found that I had created the world's longest book title! A reason enough for Horace to throw a party, but his celebration is a little more complicated...

John Hemming-Clark, Chislehurst

"I know it means Charlie doubling back, but I think it's better if he calls for you," said his mother as Horace stood by the front door in his newly ironed scout shirt and activity trousers. Horace had inspected the shirt carefully and couldn't find any needle marks, so assumed that it was new and not Sam's old one. However, when he had asked his mother earlier she had replied, "newish," so he wasn't too sure. After all, new shirts routinely came with creases across the front where they had been folded and no one would normally have bothered to iron those out, would they? When he had had another look he found that on the name tags someone had written "H Horrise" but the "H"s looked suspiciously like dollar $ signs with an extra downstroke, as if someone had started with an "S" and added a couple of down lines to vertically cross the "S" off. If someone was writing an "H", Horace decided, they couldn't do them very well because both name tags were almost identical. Nevertheless, he wasn't going to say anything. He had been grounded for most of the week, apart from school, due to recent events, and tonight was his first night of freedom after what seemed like a very, very long time although it had only been for a few days.

"I'm off, mum," said Horace as he spied Charlie walking up the front path.

"Wait there!" commanded a voice from the kitchen. Horace's mother emerged into the hallway as Charlie reached the front door and looked quizzically at Horace through the glass. "You can open it," she said, and once open she told Charlie to "Walk him straight up to scouts and walk him straight back down again."

"A bit like The Grand Old Duke of York," complained Horace with a sigh.

"Yes, Mrs Horrise," said Charlie ignoring Horace's sarcasm.

The two boys set off together on what Mrs Horrise hoped would be a shorter, quicker and much less eventful journey than Horace's solo attempt the previous week.

"So, what happened?" asked Charlie as soon as they had rounded the first corner. Although Horace had recounted the story several times at school during the week, Charlie was going to be the first to get a guided tour as well.

"I went in there with my rope," Horace said, nodding in the direction of the allotments. "Hi, Vera!" he called out, waving at an imaginary person behind the padlocked gate. "Look at what I did to the gate, that was all my own work," said Horace to Charlie, proudly pointing at the blue polypropylene rope temporarily wrapped and lashed neatly round post and gate.

"Why do they need a locked gate at all?" asked Charlie, somewhat perplexed. "After all, it's only fruit and vegetables and flowers and bamboo canes and plastic sheeting and stuff. Who's going to steal that?" Horace considered the large shed with its vast assortment of gardening implements, strimmer, shredder and ride-on lawn-mower and imagined the door being left open at night and a large notice put on the gate saying, "Help yourself!"

"My goodness!" Horace thought, "There are enough tools in that shed for each family in Chislehurst to have one each and still have some left over!"

"It's, err, to keep the kangaroos in," Horace said finally but with a limited degree of conviction.

"Kangaroos?" asked Charlie suspiciously, scrunching up his nose. "Why do they have kangaroos in the allotments?"

"One of the old men breeds them to make into burgers and steaks for The Lion's Head, but 'cos they're quite vicious they have to keep them behind a locked gate in case they escape."

"Well, Horace, I think you're talking rubbish 'cos if they're vicious then they're going to attack Vera and all the old men in there aren't they, like the tigers at the zoo that sometimes eat the keepers?" Horace considered this fairly rational argument at some length as the pair continued their walk up the road. Were kangaroos so vicious that they would harm people? Probably. So why wouldn't the allotment holders be harmed?

"The reason," Horace concluded, "is that, unlike tigers, kangaroos can be tamed so that they don't attack people that they know, like the people on the allotment."

"But they can't know everyone on the allotment."

"Well I suppose when they're new they sort of have to be kind of have to be introduced - sort of," said Horace desperate to counter each of Charlie's arguments and spectacularly failing.

"'Introduced?' To a kangaroo?" Charlie thought that his friend was pushing hard at the bounds of credibility.

"Yes."

"Were you introduced?" Horace wanted to say "No" and that because he was accompanied he was safe, but that wasn't half as interesting as "Yes", so naturally he said, "Yes!" without thinking through the consequences of such a startling admission.

"Who were you introduced to?"

"'Eric.' Eric is the main kangaroo. A bit like Skip in scouts. He's the daddy. He's in charge. He bounced over to see me and I shook his hand. He even let me have a ride in his pouch," said Horace warming to his theme.

However, this final comment put Charlie on firmer ground. "Daddy kangaroos don't have pouches unless they're wearing underpants, only the mummies have pouches."

Horace was unfazed. "Well, he was a mummy kangaroo then but just with a daddy name, probably 'cos he, she, is so big. Maybe its name was 'Erica', I don't know. After all, you're called 'Charlie' but you could be a girl 'cos there are girl Charlies like short for 'Charlotte' or 'Char..', 'Char...', well just 'Charlotte'. Most names can be boys or girls when they're shortened."

"Well 'Horace' can't be 'cos it can't be shortened."

"I could be 'Ace,'" said Horace, desperate to have the last word.

"But you're not. However, we could call you 'Hor,'" said Charlie decisively. But Horace was still determined to have the final word on the matter.

"Well who's ever heard of anyone called 'Hor?' How many girls d'you know who are 'Hors?'"

The talk of names had only temporarily knocked Charlie off course. He was still understandably sceptical about Eric, but his exchange with Horace had taken them up the road, over the next, past the first church and then they were standing on the corner opposite The Lion's Head. "And that's where they serve kangaroo!" Horace stated with a sweep of his hand, intending the kangaroo conversation to finally stop there - but it didn't. For just at that moment, having seen Horace through the pub window, the landlord came and stood on the front doorstep and waved at Horace. Horace waved nervously back.

"You okay, Horace?" the landlord called across the road.

"Yes, thank you," Horace replied quietly as he tried to usher Charlie over the road and around the corner of the building. He needn't have worried.

"Had any good kangaroo steaks recently!?" the landlord asked, smiling.

Horace smiled back and shook his head. "Come on, Charlie. We're going to be late," he said, putting his hand behind Charlie's back and pushing him keenly across the road and onto the further pavement from The Lion's Head. Horace definitely did not want to engage in any protracted conversation with the landlord although Charlie did. For he was astounded. They really did serve kangaroos in the Lion's Head.

"Did you eat kangaroo there last Friday?"

"Yes, of course. It was delicious," said Horace, justifying the lie on the grounds that kangaroo would be classed as steak and Horace had had steak, just not a kangaroo one. In any event, Charlie's scepticism had melted away in an instant. He was now going back in his mind to the conversation that the two of them had just had and the doubts that he had had. Finally Charlie asked the one remaining question that had been troubling him.

"Why don't the kangaroos just bounce over the gates?" But Horace had had time to think through most of the answers to the questions that he was inevitably going to get at the scout hut, of which this was one, so he was ready.

"The old men clip their wings like with chickens."

"But kangaroos don't have wings."

"No, I know," said Horace with a sigh. "They don't clip their wings, just like their wings. I don't know what they clip exactly, just... something... something that stops them bouncing. Chickens have wings that make them fly and kangaroos can bounce 'cos they have, um, bouncy bits - you know, a bit like a pogo-stick."

But Charlie didn't know and much to Horace's relief they had by now reached the scout hut and entered. John was folding up a flag on a rope. A number of scouts had already arrived and were running around wildly. "Hi, Skip," said Charlie approaching John. "I've brought my friend Horace along. I say his name's 'Horace' but he wants to be known as 'Hor.'"

John turned and held out his left hand. "I think we'll stick with 'Horace'. It's far more appropriate."

"Why's that then, Skip?" That was one thing John liked about Charlie. Many of his scouts, but especially Charlie, were often very inquisitive. Through their scouting activities they were taught to ask questions if they needed to as well as try to think things through for themselves. Charlie was latching on fast, but he appeared to have asked a question too far. John was smart. Like most scout leaders he tried at all times to stay one step ahead of the inevitable question, but even he was occasionally caught out by one that he didn't see coming.

"Because 'Horace' suits him. And it suits him because his name means 'Timekeeper.'"

"In that case, Skip, we should be calling him 'Badhorace.'"

"Indeed," said John, "but he's here now. Welcome, Horace, welcome. That only took you a couple of weeks. Welcome to 3rd Chislehurst. Left hand, Horace, left hand."

"Fine," said Horace, "but why?"

Already John had realised that he had another good scout in the making. Horace wasn't prepared just to hold out his left hand, he wanted to know why. But John wasn't so sure himself.

"I don't actually know, Horace. It's an old Baden-Powell thing. But we all do it in scouts."

"It's just a bit odd, that's all," said Horace seriously. "'Cos in some countries like I think like Australia and places that are miles away and so do things differently they shake hands

9

with their right hand and eat with their right hand and wipe their bottom with their left."

"Well, that won't be a problem in scouts, Horace," said John calmly.

"But I would go and check that out when you get home, Horace," he continued, giving Horace the opportunity to find out for himself whether he was correct or not.

"However, even if someone is wiping their bottom with their hand, they will usually have some sheets of toilet paper in between for during plus plenty of soap and hot water for after. Don't worry, we'll talk you through hygiene before we get near any food. Did you get here okay with Charlie? No, er, diversions?"

"No diversions, Skip" said Charlie, butting in. "But I learnt a few things. Did you know that they serve kangaroo at The Lion's Head?"

"No I didn't, Charlie," said John, before Horace could open his mouth, although it was by no means certain that he was going to, "but kangaroo meat is very low in fat, so it's quite good for you. Now I'm going to ask you a 'Did you know...?' Did you know that groups of kangaroos are called 'patrols' like we have in the scout section?"

"No, Skip. Maybe I should be in kangaroo patrol instead of Ravens."

"No, Charlie, we'll stick with the birds." John looked up, clapped his hands and gathered the scouts in a horseshoe shape in front of him ready to start the meeting, just as

Charlie was about to mention the kangaroos that supposedly lived on the allotments up the road.

"This is Horace," said John, with his hand on Horace's shoulder, once the scouts had quietened down.

"He's starting with us this term although he missed last week because he was, er, unavoidably detained. He's already our chief fundraiser nevertheless. But he's here now and he's going in Ravens patrol which is over there," John said, pointing in front of him. "So off you go and 'welcome'. We'll just have five minutes to talk about ourselves within our patrols, just to get to know each other, especially Horace and some of the other newer ones. Then, once we reconvene, we'll each say one thing that we've learnt about another scout. Go."

Horace decided to steer well away from kangaroos and spent much of the five minutes trying to memorise the names of his fellow patrol members, some of whom he knew, some he didn't. He obviously knew Charlie and he also knew Emily from school. Then there was Edward, Melanie who was assistant patrol leader and finally Archie, who was patrol leader. The patrol gelled almost immediately. "This is such fun!" said Horace, "and we've hardly started! It's a pity scouts is only once a week."

"We could meet at other times," said Archie, "now we have a great patrol. It's not a problem. We can still do scouting things and then we can earn more badges. We can call ourselves after our patrol. Let's meet tomorrow in the churchyard. You know what patrol we are, don't you Horace?"

"Yes. Skip said 'Ravings.'"

"Yeah, something like that," replied Archie. "It's 'Ravens' though."

"I thought 'Ravings' was a funny name for a bird," said Horace, wishing that he'd said something when he first heard the word.

"But Archie, I quite like 'Ravings,'" said Melanie.

"You would, Mel, with all your ramblings. But yes, we'll call ourselves 'Ravings' from now on. I think it's quite cool. Skip won't even realise if we call ourselves 'Ravings' at troop meetings. Anyway, he calls Woodpeckers 'Woods.'"

"He can't really call them 'Peckers' though can he?" suggested Edward.

"Why not?"

"'Cos a pecker is a, um..." Edward's bravado had quickly deserted him resulting in his not being able to say the word he wanted to. But Horace came to his aid.

"Person who pecks?"

"If you say so," said Edward. Then John's whistle blew - just in time.

The scouts reassembled and each was asked to say something about their neighbour in their patrol. Horace looked at Charlie, "What are you going to say about me?" he whispered but received no reply.

Horace listened intently to what the other scouts were saying, but he was hardly taking any of it in, until it was Charlie's turn. Most of the comments that had gone before were fairly tame. They included such innocuous topics as favourite food, favourite drink, favourite colour. Horace had even tried to whisper to Charlie that his favourite drink was hot chocolate but to no avail. When Skip asked Charlie to give the scouts a snippet about Horace he cleared his throat, lifted his head up and announced loudly and clearly, "Horace has had a ride in a kangaroo's pouch." And then, as if to seal his fate added, "In Chislehurst!" However, despite Horace's immediate concerns no one laughed or even gasped. In fact the scouts appeared to be very impressed and there was plenty of nodding with affirmative noises being made. "When?" they wanted to know. "Last Friday," said Charlie, "on the allotments." Suddenly the mood changed from one of admiration to one of disbelief. Horace went bright red and the scouts fell silent. They were all thinking the same thing, "Who on earth is this 'Horace' nutter?" It was a question that would be asked at regular intervals over the next few years.

Raving Horace Horrise had arrived. Horace Horrise, Raving, had arrived. Horace Horrise had arrived Raving. Whatever way it was written it was true.

***

Horace's mother was looking anxiously out of the sitting room window when Charlie and Horace finally came into view. She glanced up at the clock. It was only a quarter past nine. The two boys walked up to the front door and were engaged in an animated discussion when Horace's mother appeared on the other side and opened it slowly not trying to look too relieved. "Oh, hallo Mrs Horrise. I've brought Horace home," said Charlie triumphantly.

"Yes, thank you very much Charlie. Are you coming in?"

"No, he's not," said Horace firmly. "When you told his mummy that he needed to walk me to scouts and back he thought he needed to bring me to the front door and then see me inside. Given half the chance he'ld be closing my curtains, making me a hot chocolate and tucking me up in bed."

"Very sensible and 'thank you' again Charlie and good night," said Horace's mother as she closed the front door. "Come into the sitting room darling and tell me all about it."

Horace went in and found a large slice of Victoria sponge waiting for him. "I thought that if something happened with Charlie, you would smell this and come straight home," she said condescendingly.

"Thank you very much, mummy, but I don't need bribing," he replied as he sat down and set about demolishing the cake. Between, as well as during, mouthfuls he told his mother about the evening's events: the other scouts, his patrol and those that were in it, and the games that they played. He also informed her that he would be invested once he had been attending for a couple of weeks or so.

"That can't all have taken two hours," said his mother looking somewhat surprised.

"It didn't mummy. I haven't told you the best bit yet. I was saving that for last. Why would I tell you the best bit first 'cos if I did you wouldn't listen to the rest of it 'cos it wouldn't be so excit..."

"Oh, for goodness sake, Horace, get on with it." His mother went and sat next to him on the sofa; she picked up her glass and smiled. It was so good to have Horace back from scouts in one piece.

"We have to earn badges for doing stuff, different stuff," he continued. "This evening we started work on our smallholders' badge. We had to dig over some of the scout hut grounds and then we had to prepare the earth for growing some vegetables over the winter and then next year we can do fruit and more vegetables and herbs as well. Then, once we've done that we have to talk it over with Skip. 'Cos there were so many of us we managed to dig it over really quickly."

Horace's mother sighed. "I wish someone would dig over some of my garden for fruit and a few more vegetables and herbs. And flowers, that would be nice."

"But mummy," Horace protested, "we have Fred. He could do that for you."

"No he can't. Well he could but he's not going to. He's quite expensive for what he does. He only really cuts and strims and generally tidies up and looks after the potatoes."

"I didn't know that we had any potatoes."

"We were growing some at the back of the garden, but they were spoiled because when he dug up the main crop recently he said that he found loads of glass in them."

"Mummy?"

"Yes, darling?" Then Horace decided that he had burdened his mother with rather too much recently, both with confessions and more general grief-inducing issues that he decided that a little cooling-off period was called for. He could tell her about the broken mirror disposal at some future date.

"Oh, it's nothing mummy." But Horace was already formulating a plan. He was not only preparing, he was shortly going to be executing. Saying "sorry" for what he had done recently would simply not be good enough. He could do more. He would do something extremely positive, something to show her that he really was sorry.

***

In the morning over breakfast Horace's mother told her children that she and their father were going to be going for a mini mini-break the following Friday evening and would be staying away for "one night only" in order that they might celebrate Horace's father's fiftieth birthday. They would be back late on Saturday evening. Whilst Horace was at scouts Sam was to look after Olivia and then Charlie's mother would bring Horace home from scouts and make sure that the three children were settled before going home. There would be plenty of food in the freezer and fridge and they were to go about their usual Saturday chores as normal.

"Any questions?"

There were none. For Horace's part his mind had switched to overdrive as he realised that his plan would be put into action sooner than he had envisaged.

The Ravings met as planned in the churchyard later in the morning. Archie had picked on that particular place as the venue because, as he had told the others, it would be really quiet. "The only other people that will be around will be dead," he assured them somewhat bluntly. However, as the six of them arrived in ones and twos they found that the place of the dead was, in fact, a hive of activity. There were a number of adults and not a few children working hard on the trees, shrubs and weeds. They were cutting, trimming, pulling and digging. Horace was impressed with their commitment. Normally appearances would be reversed, but as the Ravings stood by near the church porch, watching the comings and goings, even the most casual of observers would have felt obliged to comment that the six that one would expect to be the dirtiest were actually very clean, whereas those whom one would think would ordinarily be extremely presentable had mud on their hands, twigs and leaves in their hair and grass clippings stuck to their boots. The first to speak was a man who introduced himself as Ray. "Hallo children," he said cheerily, "have you come to help?"

"We're not sure," said Archie, taking up the role of Raving spokesman and not wishing to talk his friends into something too onerous. "What are you doing?"

Ray laughed, which the Ravings considered a most unnecessary response to Archie's perfectly reasonable question. "Gardening!" he replied, as if he were making a statement of the obvious. "We meet up once a month to look after the churchyard. It would be quite expensive to pay someone so we all do a bit each. 'Many hands make light work' and all that. Probably Biblical. Not sure. Anyway, would you like to help? There are plenty of tools in the shed."

"Does it have a bar in it like Horace's dad's?" asked Charlie, assuming that such fittings were the norm in Chislehurst's outbuildings. Ray laughed again, but before he could answer Archie interrupted.

"No, I don't think that we will be able to help today as we're having a planning meeting 'cos we've just met for the first time outside of scouts," he said firmly.

"So you're scouts are you?" Ray asked, looking hopeful. "What about the Scout Promise that talks about doing your duty to God? You could do your duty this morning by helping, couldn't you?"

"I haven't been invested yet," said Horace, playing for time.

"All the more reason to prepare yourself for when you are," said Ray who seemed to have a response to everything. There was no point trying to wriggle out of the situation that they found themselves almost in. It was to be a case of helping or simply running away.

"Come on," implored Ray. "Horace's dad's shed sounds like a proper shed, but 'no', ours doesn't have a bar. However, in about an hour's time we have elevenses, more like twelveses actually, but it's worth hanging around for or should I say, working towards. We have squash and buns and cakes and..."

"We'll stay," said Horace before Archie could continue going down on what Horace at that point considered the wrong track.

"Whoa, you're not patrol leader," said Emily holding her hands up in front of her in an attempt to shield herself against any fallout from the metaphorical attack that she felt that Archie was under.

"No, I'm not," said Horace, "but I don't expect Archie is going to say 'no' to cake and buns are you Archie?" But Archie didn't hear - he was already halfway to the churchyard shed to acquaint himself with a trowel.

Ray split the Ravings up into three pairs. Horace and Charlie were given the task of digging up a large quantity of daffodil bulbs and redistributing them to various new positions in the churchyard. "Don't dig too deep, Charlie," implored Horace as they started on their work, "in case you dig up a body."

"I don't think that's very likely Horace. They bury bodies hundreds of feet down to stop them escaping," said Charlie knowledgably.

"They're not going to escape when they're dead are they?" reasoned Horace.

"No, but imagine if the people who decide if you're dead get it wrong and you're just asleep then it's going to look very bad on them if they bury you and then you wake up and you're only a couple of feet underground and you start knocking on your coffin. Then someone would hear and dig you out and someone else would be in big trouble, wouldn't they? So just to make sure they bury you a long way down so that if you do wake up you're more likely to be stuffed 'cos you would die anyway then unless you could get your hands on some water to drink and some worms to eat."

Pointing to the ground Horace asked, "So do you think that there are people in this churchyard down there that are still alive?"

"Possibly. Look at this grave for instance. It says 'Here Lieth Arnold John Grieve. Died 8th October 1876, aged 47.' That means he's been down there for years and years and years.

Horace looked pensive. "He'ld have had to have eaten a lot of worms, probably bucketfuls to stay alive." Astonishingly, in all their wild imaginings, the fact that had Arnold John Grieve been buried alive and survived all the intervening years and would by then be well on his way to his one hundred and fiftieth birthday, was completely lost on this pair of dyscalculians.

"Look, whatever's going on deep down there, we're only digging down a few inches, so we should be okay." And with that they put their collective heads down and continued with their unplanned labouring.

The rest of the morning passed extremely quickly. Ray didn't appear to do an awful lot of work himself, the Ravings noted; instead he satisfied himself by wandering round the various small groups and encouraging them in their endeavours. The Ravings all met back up by the porch along with more adults and children than they had previously realised were at work in the churchyard. "I bet some of them have just turned up for the cake," thought Horace as he tried to count the number of individuals then the number of cakes and buns on an enormous tray that

Ray was holding. He didn't think that there were enough. "Better get in first, although that may look a little greedy," he thought. He needn't have worried.

"I would like to introduce six scouts from 3rd Chislehurst who are helping us this morning," said Ray to the gardeners, as he helped himself to the first fairy cake with his free hand whilst balancing the tray on his other. He started to eat the cake without attempting to peel the wrapper off first, diving in from the top with his mouth open wide. At least there wouldn't be much washing up. "I think they're doing a fabulous job and we hope to see them again," he said encouragingly, spitting out crumbs of soggy sponge over the ornate tiled floor. "In the meantime you can have first dibs on the cakes, scouts."

"But after you Ray," said one of the adults and everyone laughed. Except Ray. He continued, "If ever you need anything doing at the scout hut, let us know and we'll see what we can do..."

"Yes, there is one thing that you can do," thought Horace. He would have a quiet word with Ray once everyone had gone back to work. In the meantime, a large jug of squash had appeared, followed by another huge tray of cakes. Things were looking up after all.

Having excelled themselves to the delight of Ray and met and chatted to many of those who turned out to be part of a regular team, as they were preparing to leave Ray said that he would give the Ravings a tour of the churchyard. They were shown the graves of people who had become quite famous, or infamous, in their lifetimes. There was a murderer, two murdered, a Member of Parliament, a poet and a world record breaker. When it was time for "Any questions?" Horace thought that he might ask Ray if any of the individuals could still be alive under all the earth, but decided against it. They were then shown the memorial garden. "This is where those who are cremated have their ashes buried," said Ray. "We try to keep it looking very neat, but with all the digging that goes on it's become a little uneven. It could really do with re-turfing but there's always a more pressing job to do and good turf costs."

"They won't be eating any worms," said Charlie assuredly.

"Why do some people get buried as bodies and some as ashes?" asked Horace.

"Good question, Horace. Mainly space," said Ray. "If you're buried you take up a couple of square meters of ground. If you're cremated then you're just half an urnful."

"'Half an 'andful?'" asked Charlie. "Mum says that Horace is a handful, and probably a whole one, not just a half." Ray did not respond so Charlie carried blissfully on.

"But if you're put in a coffin and you're not dead at least you'll still be alive if you're buried. If you're set on fire then you will definitely be dead," he reasoned, keen to salvage a smidgen of credibility with Horace, and hoping that Ray would at least acknowledge the possibility of Charlie's comment having some merit. His hopes were to be dashed.

"I can assure you, Charlie, that by the time you get to be put in a coffin you will definitely be dead."

"Let's hope so," said Horace. "Can you imagine when they have the service for you and all your friends are there and you're in the middle of the church like when you're getting married but you're not 'cos you're lying down and hidden. Even so probably people wear the same posh clothes. Then as the vicar says, 'We're sorry that Horace has died,' and then there's a 'knock, knock, knock' on the coffin lid followed by 'Let me out! It's not funny!' That would be a bit of a shock for everyone wouldn't it and probably a good enough reason not ever to play hide and seek in a long wooden box?"

"It would probably mean that there would be a few more funerals shortly after for some of the mourners, if that were to happen, Horace," said Ray gravely.

"Hmm, yes," said Horace. "Probably better to keep quiet then and look forward to a diet of worms."

The morning had been a very successful one for the Ravings, if somewhat unplanned. Horace had his quiet word, but there was more to do. The members dispersed for lunch with an injunction to meet back outside the allotments in two hours' time.

"Had a good morning, darling?" asked his mother when Horace returned home and before he had even shut the front door. He bounced into the sitting room and dived onto the sofa sideways over one of the arms.

"Can't you just sit on it darling?" implored his mother wearily.

"I could mummy," but today I'm coffin-surfing. I'm trying to see how you could get into a coffin accidently. I don't think it would be too easy."

"Darling, I don't know what you're talking about, but I hope you've been having fun."

"Yes, thank you, mummy. I've been busy in the churchyard digging up bulbs."

"Yes, darling, of course you have. I can see you've been doing some sort of manual work, but I hope you weren't stealing anything."

"No mummy, we were helping the church people. But mummy...?"

"Yes darling?" Horace's mother readied herself for yet another confession, revelation, admission or request. However, on this occasion it was merely a question, albeit an unusual one.

"Mummy, is it possible to live on worms?" Horace's mother had become quite used to his rather esoteric questioning over the years so was completely unfazed by his worm wonderings, even though she wasn't completely sure of the answer.

"Possibly. For a while at least. But you would need more in your diet than just worms. And given that they're so slippery they would probably just disappear down your throat without you having the opportunity to chew them so your teeth would become redundant over a longer period of time and fall out. Then you wouldn't be able to chew anything, even if you wanted to. Also, when you're eating the worm, you're eating the earth that they've been in and all their internal organs unless you're going to clean them first." Horace's mother paused for a moment. She thought that maybe she had gone a little too far in her explanation;

maybe she was starting to sound a little like Horace with talk of rotten teeth and innards. It was time to call a halt to her explanation and to pass the matter back to Horace.

"Actually I would imagine that they would just wriggle straight through you and out the other end. Why do you ask?" But Horace wasn't playing his mother's game.

"No reason mummy, just wondering."

***

The Ravings met back up in the afternoon as planned. Arriving one by one they observed the comings and goings of the various allotment holders. Each individual carefully unlocked the gate, entered or exited and then locked it up again. There was not one person who left the gate open or unlocked with the result that even Archie was beginning to imagine that there were kangaroos behind the gate. However, so intent was Horace on securing the second part of his plan that he had completely forgotten about what he had said about kangaroos to Charlie and what Charlie had said about kangaroos to the scout troop.

Horace was the last to arrive. "Let's go!" he announced and they crossed the road together. At the gate they hesitated whilst Horace tried to get someone's attention but to no avail. Eventually a man walked up to the gate from inside with a bag of potatoes in one hand and a pumpkin under one arm.

"Can I help you?" the man inquired as he unlocked the gate. Evidently he was not one of the male equivalents of a damsel in distress from the other day.

"We've come to help on the allotments," announced Archie.

"Really?" asked the man, sounding as though this were not a very common request.

Horace tried another tack. "Yes, yes. Vera's expecting us."

"Oh, right, um, okay." The man was evidently thinking that he was going to have to put down his produce, unlock the gate, let the six Ravings in, accompany them to the shed, find Vera, return to the gate and resume from where he was standing, all of which was going to take several minutes – minutes that he didn't appear to have spare. He looked the Ravings up and down. It certainly appeared as though they had been doing some gardening. "Have you been here earlier?"

Horace knew that this could possibly be a trap. How could Horace know whether this man had been there earlier himself and so would know the answer? Horace decided to play it safe. "Not today. We were helping at the churchyard this morning. It's the turn of the allotments in the afternoon."

"Right. Yes. Um. Do you know where to find Vera?"

"Yes of course. She's probably in the shed. That's where I normally find her." Horace was convinced that he had avoided telling a lie. The shed was where he had found Vera before, the fact that he had only been once before and none of the others had been at all was rather glossed over. In any case the explanation was obviously sufficient for the man as he let them all in before he then left, locking the gate behind him. The Ravings stood quite still, looking around, lest Eric should come bounding over with an evil glint in his eye, but the only animal they could see was a whippet halfway down the main path, its lead wrapped round a fork that had been buried in the earth.

Horace led the Ravings up to the shed and peeked inside. Vera was not there but a couple of old men were. "Excuse me, but I'm looking for Vera. Do you know where she might be?" asked Horace politely.

"She's working on her allotment, sunshine," said one.

"'Sitting on' more like," said the other, and they both laughed. When Horace didn't move, one said, "Turn round, go left fifty yards and you'll see her."

Once more Horace led the way until the six of them came to the allotment that was unmistakably Vera's, with grass, fruit trees and a deckchair in the middle, just as she had described. Snuggled inside the deckchair with a mug of tea on the grass on one side and an opened book with pages down on the other was - a man! "Excuse me, please," said Horace from the edge of the grass, not sure whether he should tread on it. An eye slowly opened.

"Yes?"

"Please, I'm sorry. I thought you were Vera."

"I've been called many things in my time, sonny, but never 'Vera.'"

"Sorry, but do you know where she is?" Then Horace added, as if to encourage the man to spill the beans, "We've come to help."

The man shifted in the deckchair, opened the other eye to get a better look at Horace, as he waved his right arm around down beside him feeling for his mug. "She'll be needing all the help she can get!" he exclaimed, laughing suddenly. "You see, we've had a bit of a change around. I've been coming to these allotments for over fifteen years and week in, week out, my wife's sat here in her back garden allotment and read her books and magazines and drank her tea and watched me weed, dig, prepare, plant, harvest, weed, dig, prepare, plant, harvest. And when the weather's not too good, she's in the shed whilst I weed, dig..."

"Do you get a cup of tea?" asked Melanie interrupting.

"Well, yes, of course, now and again."

"And a biscuit?"

"Yes."

"And who makes your packed lunch when you're up here for the day?"

"Er..."

"And who makes you your tea when you go home in the evening?"

"And who's washing and ironing and folding and changing beds and washing up and, and, and, er, stuff?" added Horace who, once he started warming to Melanie's theme, rapidly ran out of chores even though there were plenty more, thus completely spoiling the point that Melanie was trying to make.

"Vera!" the Ravings shouted in unison.

"Er, yes, yes, you're right," said the man. "I'll just go and fetch her," whereupon he began to lever himself out of the deckchair in the rather comical way that most adults get out of deckchairs – and that is with a bit of a struggle, as if someone has tried to temporarily glue them to the material. He need not have bothered. The sound of six young people shouting your name would wake that person up from half a mile away; as it was Vera was no more than fifty yards away, on the neighbouring plot, on hands and knees, trying to dig out some bindweed. Grateful for an excuse to stop for a few minutes she came over and smiled at Horace and his friends. No longer in her smart summer dress, her attire looked more like that of the men from the churchyard in the morning.

"Hallo, Horace. I didn't think we'ld see you back so soon." Before Horace could answer, Edward had a pressing question and it couldn't wait, lest he forgot, albeit unlikely.

"Do you think that I could ask you a question please?"

"Of course you can. What would you like to know?"

"Could you tell me where the kangaroos are please?" Edward had fixed it in his head that if these kangaroos were real then he would have seen them in the shed or bouncing around the allotments as if he were wandering through the Australian grasslands or a safari park. Vera was not one to be fazed by such a question, however. She had had children of her own and she knew that to play along with their fantasies was an excellent way to develop their imaginations. Horace, however, feared the worst. His frenzied imagination portrayed as truth was just about to be uncovered.

"I'm afraid they're not here today."

"Where are they?"

"Where do you think they are?" Edward shook his head.

"The ones that aren't very well have gone to hospital for a hoperation; the others have gone to Bromley sh-hopping." Vera smiled at Edward gently. She thought that she had been quite successful in her reply, and that the Ravings would appreciate it. Evidentially not. Apart from Horace who sighed heavily.

"Oh," said Edward, then fell silent.

"So, what can I do for you all? Horace?"

"We've come to help. As scouts we are expected to get involved in community projects and working on the allotments is almost the same thing. So we were wondering whether some of the old men would like us to help them with their plots."

"They're not all old, Horace," said Vera with a smile, "but some of them are quite lazy. Like that, for instance," she said, pointing over to her husband, who had given up on his struggle with the deckchair and had slumped back down and closed his eyes once more.

"I thought you told Horace that your husband was the one doing all the digging?" said Edward.

"Oh, he does normally, but he hates digging up bindweed. You have to dig every single little bit up, and it's so fiddly and he really detests doing it, so I said that I would do it and he could be in charge of making teas which I'm sure he'll do fine – it's just that he hasn't started yet."

The Ravings stood silently contemplating the life of a retired man sitting in his "garden" and making cups of tea – it wasn't very appealing. Vera broke the silence. "Come on then, if you want to do some work. I'll certainly find you some things to do. How much time do you have? Do you want to work as a team or pairs or individually?" After the morning's pairings the Ravings thought it would be more fun to work as a team. "Okay," said Vera. Go round the back of the shed and find yourself a wheelbarrow each. Then go into the shed and ask whoever's in there for a small spade each and a large roll of black bags. Then come and find me by the entrance gate.

Down past the Ravings' scout hut was a stables. It had been there for years. One of the problems that the stables used to have was what to do with the copious amounts of horse manure that was regularly piled up in the yard. An arrangement was eventually made with the allotment holders that once a month Mr Cox, the stable owner, would pile the manure up on the back of his large old wooden trailer and arrange for it to be tractored down to the allotments where it would be dumped. No money ever changed hands although the tractor driver would occasionally return to the stables with a bag of plums or a few apples. Normally the arrival of the "turd trailer," as the gardeners somewhat crudely called it, would lead to, if not quite a stampede, a period of frenzied activity as the various plot holders barrowed manure from the pile to their individual allotments where it was squirreled away under tarpaulin for a few months or over the winter and left to rot some more before digging into the ground to add vital nutrients to the soil. Being a casual arrangement, there was no fixed date or time for each delivery. It would simply turn up "as and when." As a result those that were there at the right time got the manure, and those that weren't didn't. It just so happened that only an hour before the Ravings had turned up there had been a delivery, and most of the pile remained untouched, dumped behind the boundary hedge by the front gate where it couldn't be seen, but could certainly be smelled, from the road.

As Vera stood by the pile of horse manure, that was almost as high as she was tall, she watched the Ravings as they picked their way through the allotments with barrows and spades. As they drew closer Charlie exclaimed, "Look at that! I didn't see that earlier."

"That's because it's hidden behind the hedge, so you can't see it from the road," said Vera as they reached her.

"But you can smell it!"

"Yes, we can't hide that. If you stood outside, on the opposite pavement and watched the gardeners come in the gate, the first thing they all do is look to the left. Someone not in the know might speculate that they are checking to make sure the kangaroo that's on guard that day isn't about to pounce, but in reality they're checking to see if there's a pile of manure ready for distributing."

So inured were the Ravings becoming to kangaroo talk that no one even thought to question Vera's statement. Instead Edward asked, "What is it?"

"It's manure, kangaroo manure. As they're all out for the day we've collected it up and put it in this pile for everyone to take. However, your task is to help everyone have an equal amount each because some try and take more than others. So what I would like you to do is fill your barrows to the top with manure, level it off, and work out in an ever increasing arc, delivering the manure to the edge of each plot, one barrow each. Deposit it in the black bags to keep the site tidy and to help the manure break down. We have loads of black bags because they can be used as overshoes when it gets really muddy.

"How do you do that?" asked Archie.

"You double-bag each lower leg and tie the bag up in a knot. When you get back to your car or home you simply take them off and your boots or shoes and trousers are mud free."

"But it stinks!" complained Emily.

"Come on," said Horace. "By the time we've finished we'll all stink the same." And with those words ringing in their ears the Ravings dug, filled, barrowed, tipped and returned for two whole hours, until the large pile had completely disappeared and mini piles had sprung up all over the allotments as if there had been a giant mole invasion.

Vera was overjoyed. "What you have done is fantastic!" she enthused. "You've helped me out no end. No squabbling this month from the gardeners. Excellent work. Come on into the shed for some refreshments, won't you?"

"Yes," said Horace, once more agreeing to something that he wasn't entirely sure what it meant but was probably, from previous experience, something advantageous. Horace looked at Archie and frowned.

"I think she means drinks," Archie whispered.

"Why doesn't she say that then? Why do adults have to use complicated words when there are easier ones that everyone can understand?"

"I think because 'refreshments' means more than just drinks, like food," said Emily. The Ravings walked a little faster. As they filed into the shed they found themselves confronted by a large jug of orange squash and a box of assorted doughnuts. Without even realising what he was doing, Horace started to count the doughnuts. There were exactly twelve. Fantastic! Two each.

"Help yourselves to a drink each, children. There are some cups over there. Now, who likes doughnuts?" Horace counted, there were seven hands in the air and no one had raised two. There were six Ravings and one Vera.

"Why is it that adults have to spoil the children's fun?" thought Horace. First it was Ray, now it was Vera. She stood in front of them holding the box and as they approached she helped herself to a triple-chocolate flavour and bit into it. But no one said anything. The Ravings took a doughnut each and within a couple of minutes they were all gone. Vera had three and the Ravings each had one and a half. Still no one said anything.

Soon it was time to leave. Some of the men appeared at the shed to thank the Ravings for all their hard work. "If ever you need something doing at the scout hut, children, just let us know and we'll see what we can do," said Vera.

"Yes, there are a couple of things that you can do," thought Horace. He would have a quiet word with Vera once the rest of the Ravings had started their homeward journeys.

***

Horace had had a busy few days so was pleased when Friday came and he could meet up with the rest of the Ravings once more. Although John had talked to them about the allotment side of the smallholders' badge, there were two other parts, farming and livestock. "We don't have to do the other parts," John told the scouts, "but I thought that it would be interesting if you learnt a little about animals other than cats, dogs and rabbits. So I've brought along Mrs Ives who keeps chickens and she's going to tell you all about how they're housed, fed and bred as well as their economic uses. She's going to show you how to handle them safely and you will also learn a little about animal welfare. We also have Mr Jones here this evening and he's going to tell you about managing a bee hive. He's brought in some honey. Over to you Mrs Ives and Mr Jones."

The pair of animal enthusiasts looked over the sea of faces and beamed. "My goodness, I recognise a few faces from the allotments! Do you Mr Jones?" asked Mrs Ives.

"I do indeed," replied Mr Jones.

"In that case, who has an allotment up the road?" asked John. No one raised their hand.

"I don't think that anyone has an allotment as such, John, but we met Horace a couple of weeks ago when he was helping us to mend our gate, and last Saturday the Ravings came and helped..."

"The who?" asked John.

"The, er..."

"The Ravens," said Archie before the situation got out of hand.

"I was sure that you were calling yourselves 'Ravings,'" said Mrs Ives, looking rather perplexed.

"It's only Horace," said Archie, who decided to sacrifice his newest patrol member for the protection of the rest. "He's saying 'Ravens' but it comes out as 'Ravings'. We don't like to correct him though as he gets very embarrassed about his impediment."

"Oh, I'm so s-sorry, I didn't mean to offend," said Mrs Ives understandingly. "Please accept my apology, Horace. As I was saying, John, Horace and a group of scouts came to the allotments last Saturday to help as part of a community enterprise I believe. They worked like Trojans, moving all the horse manure..."

"Kangaroo manure," said Melanie. "It was kangaroo manure. Vera said so."

"Oh, well, yes, I see, I'm so sorry. Oh gosh, I seem to be spending my time apologising. I really didn't realise. I never need any myself as I have enough manure from my chickens, you see." Mr Jones looked more than a little perplexed himself but didn't feel that he could interrupt.

"Maybe we have horse and kangaroo manure. In any event the six scouts moved a huge pile of something..."

"Oh we know what it is," said Emily interrupting, "it's shi..."

"And we are all so grateful," said Mrs Ives, wrestling the conversation back to where it belonged. "Anyway, I came to talk about my chickens. Maybe one day some of you would like to keep a few."

After her slightly faltering start Mrs Ives talked at length about the mechanics of keeping chickens to the delight of the scouts who maintained a respectful silence, listening to her every word. Towards the end of her talk she went out to her car and returned holding a large cardboard box with holes punched through it. She opened up the flaps on the top and put the box on the floor. All of a sudden the most enormous chicken almost jumped out. It flapped its wings and flew up onto a chair seat. It flapped its wings again and managed to get itself onto the back of the chair where it perched quite happily. It surveyed the scouts who were sitting on the floor; it looked as though it was regarding them as pieces of corn and was wondering which one it would peck first. "It" soon became a "he" because Mrs Ives said that this magnificent specimen of pure Rhode Island Red who was called Albert was, in fact, a cockerel. As if on cue Albert threw back his head and let out a full throttle "cock-a-doodle-doo!" The scouts were entranced; Horace was wide-eyed with fascination. He had never been so close to a cockerel before. Mrs Ives then told the scouts that sadly Albert couldn't stay on the allotments much longer as he was nearly fully grown and would be disturbing too many of the "local stuck-up residents who don't know where an egg comes from" so he would "have to leave." Unfortunately Mrs Ives didn't manage to get away with that little

37

genteelism because Melanie then asked where Albert would be going.

"Well, I'm not sure at this stage, but we'll find somewhere for him." Mrs Ives was keen not to say, "in the oven, plucked and gutted with a chopped-up onion and a few springs of rosemary down his throat" but neither did she want to lie. "Wherever it is, I'm sure that he'll be nice and warm." She dared not look over in John's direction. "So that's all for now. I'll be off and thank you for listening and I hope it's been useful, but Albert has to go back to the allotment and consider his future." During the respectful round of applause that followed and whilst Albert was being put back in his box, Horace went over to Mrs Ives and asked,

"Do you think I could have a quick word?"

Next up was Mr Jones. He kept the scouts equally enthralled having brought along some honeycomb and honey. He showed the scouts how to use a smoker and explained how it was able to calm the bees when he needed to extract the honey or inspect them. He showed the scouts a wooden hive and started to unclip the lid. "What about all the bees?" asked Emily uneasily, "Won't they escape?"

"Or did you leave them at home 'cos they hadn't been beehiving, ha, ha?" asked Horace cheekily.

"Fortunately there are no bees in this hive," said Mr Jones, ignoring Horace's question, "otherwise you would have up to sixty thousand of them buzzing around your scout hut. However this hive is not being used at present."

Finally Mr Jones unscrewed the lid from a jar of honey and the scouts were all allowed to dip a finger in and "taste a foodstuff that never goes mouldy." Once again, the speaker was given a polite round of applause and Horace asked if he could carry Mr Jones' hive out to the car for him, an offer which Mr Jones gratefully accepted.

After Charlie's mother had ensured that Horace was safely indoors with his brother and sister for the night and she had returned home, Horace announced that he just had to pop next door to Susie's to "sort out a small matter". He was back within ten minutes. "Sorted!" he told Sam. Sam took no notice.

***

Saturday started unusually early for Horace. Olivia was perfectly malleable but Sam less so. However, he needn't have worried. At eight o'clock in the morning, just as Horace was getting out of bed without, for once, his mother's assistance, Sam bounded into his bedroom and announced that he was going out for the day. "I'm going round to Tanya's and we're going up to London. There's food in the fridge and you're to look after Olivia. I'll be back in twelve hours."

Horace wanted to remonstrate but it was distinctly to his advantage not to. He did mention to Sam that maybe eleven was a bit too young to be looking after a younger sister but Sam said, "Don't panic, Horace. Mum and dad decided that I'm old enough to be put in charge and that hasn't changed. I'm just that I'm not old enough to realise that it's not a good idea to leave you two alone. But that's not my problem as I'm under eighteen and therefore not responsible for my actions. Anyway, I am still in charge, just not in charge here, in charge whilst I'm somewhere else, that's all."

Horace would normally be at least a match for his brother's verbal dexterity but he still wasn't quite awake and so any attempt to counter Sam's rather irrational justification for leaving his two siblings alone for the day was doomed to failure. Nevertheless he tried. "But if you say that you're not old enough to realise that it's not a good idea to leave us two alone then you must know that it's not," he said.

Sam however wasn't going to argue. He had Tanya on his mind. "Whatever." And on that final word, Sam was off.

No sooner had Horace sat down to a breakfast of chips and ice cream than there was a knock at the door. It was Ray. "Good morning," said Ray with almost a smile. "Here I am, returning the help. It's what community is all about. I hope you have cake!"

"Oh, hi, Ray," said Horace cheerfully. "It really is very good of you to come and help. I didn't think I was going to need you quite so soon. Come round to the back of the house and I'll see you there."

By the time that Horace had found his footwear, put it on and opened the back door, Ray was already standing on the patio looking at the back garden with a group of about thirty of his churchyard helpers. "It's quite a big lawn," said Ray cautiously.

"It's about ten metres by twenty-five roughly. I don't need you to dig it though as I said, just cut it into strips then across with your spades so that each bit is two feet by four feet."

"My goodness," said Ray. You do make it difficult for yourself! Why don't you stick to metric or imperial - metres and centimetres or feet and inches?"

"It's no problem," said Horace. I can do both. Big stuff like gardens is metric and really big stuff like roads is miles. But little stuff is best with feet and inches 'cos I can measure stuff with my body, like my feet for feet and my thumb for inches. That's what they did in the old days. The only thing is I'm not grown up yet so my foot isn't quite a foot and my thumb isn't quite an inch but you can measure the lawn with your feet and we should be okay."

"Well I'm glad we've got that sorted out, Horace," said Ray with a dramatic sigh.

"Then," Horace continued, "get your spades about three inches underneath and dig along but not down until the bits of lawn are all wobbly. Leave a little verge either end to walk along, beside the path on one side and the border on the other. Then roll up the bits of lawn nice and neatly and put them by the pavement out the front. Susie needs a good few next door for repairs and you can have what you need for the memorial garden. The rest are going to the allotments 'cos Vera said that they're always needing to replace bits of grass 'here and there'."

"Gosh, Horace. You know what you want, don't you?" said Ray, who was by then thinking of other projects the Ravens could get involved in at the churchyard.

"I've been busy at the allotments recently," said Horace somberly, "so I know what's what. And I'm going to get my smallholders' badge before I've even been invested."

The churchyard gardeners worked hard and fast. So much so that by lunchtime the Horrise back lawn had completely disappeared, leaving just soil and stones. On the pavement at the front of the house lay around two hundred turves with one hundred having already been delivered to Susie next door and which some of the churchyard workers were busy laying for her. Horace went to inspect the remaining pile with Ray just as Mr Cox from the stables arrived on his tractor chugging down the road. "Fifty to the memorial garden in the churchyard and the rest to the allotments please. And then, cake and tea for everyone on the lawn on the, um, front garden," Horace announced.

As if on cue Olivia appeared at the front door with a large tea tray piled high with cake. Behind her followed a couple of the churchyard workers who had made mugs of tea and coffee. "This is fantastic cake," said Ray who had already rushed over and taken two pieces, but before he had even taken a bite out of one. "You certainly know how to live in Holbrook Road don't you?"

"It's not always this fantastic," explained Horace apologetically, "but mummy and daddy have gone away to give us time to redo the back garden, 'cos that's what mummy wanted. Sam's supposed to be looking after us but he's gone out with his girlfriend but we can manage 'cos we're scouts, well nearly, and Olivia's a cub. Mummy told us that there is loads of food in the fridge and freezer. When we had a look last night the fridge was a bit dull 'cos there was tons of green stuff, although there is enough Champagne in the wet fridge to launch a whole fleet of ships but I don't think that that's for me. In the freezer where there's usually stuff in pots and sandwich bags that's all iced up and no one knows what it is 'cos it's been there for years, we found millions of ice cubes to keep the Champagne cold. Then we found three cakes in cake tins all hidden away in the saucepan cupboard so that the adults could have it all to themselves, oink oink, but I don't think so and we won't get into trouble 'cos when we ate the Mars bars that we found in the secret-shed secret-fridge we didn't and anyway the cakes will do the trick 'cos we know you all like cake don't we Ray?!"

"Well, just say 'thank you' to your parents when they return. It's been a pleasure to help you, Horace and we hope to see you up at the churchyard before too long with the rest of your pals." Ray gathered up his tools and his workers and they were off.

"That went well, Olivia," said Horace with a satisfied look on his face as he closed the front door. "Now we just have time for a quick sandwich before the afternoon action. Or shall we just have cake ourselves?"

***

At precisely two o'clock Horace and Olivia were standing by their front gate, waiting expectantly. "I can hear them," said Olivia after a couple of minutes.

Sure enough there was the unmistakable sound of a band of out of tune adults singing, "Hi, ho, hi, ho, it's off to work we go..." as around fifty individuals rounded the corner at the end of the road and came into view. At the front was Vera, followed by her merry mostly men pushing wheelbarrows containing tools, bamboo sticks, string and two large machines that looked like lawn mowers with the casings removed.

"Which way, Horace?" asked Vera, without stopping.

"Hi Vera, a few to sweep the pavement mess and the rest up the side please."

Horace and Olivia followed the back garden detail round to the patio. Two of the men were already starting up the machinery with plenty of huffing and puffing.

"What are those things?" asked Horace curiously.

"You need the ground digging over, don't you?" demanded one of the men.

"Yes please," said Horace politely, "but I thought that you would use forks and spades and things."

"Maybe we would if we were doing a few spuds," said the man. "But we have a serious amount of ground here to sort out."

"It's the same size as an allotment," said Horace slightly perplexed and not a little concerned at what he guessed was just about to happen. After all it wasn't a hole for a swimming pool that he wanted digging out.

"Indeed. So we use these chaps. They're called rotavators. You know when you see tractors digging over the ground ready for planting? They use a big tilling device on the back that turns over the earth. These chaps do the same thing, only they're much smaller and one-man. Watch."

The man stood at one corner of the ground and held onto the rotavator as its blades spun wildly round then started to bury itself like a hermit crab hiding from its predators.

Then the rotavator started to move down the line. Another man worked next to the first and soon they were walking up and down the area with the rotavators expertly turning over the soil. Whilst Horace was watching with his eyes transfixed on the back garden being remodelled but not completely excavated before his eyes, Vera came up to him and showed him "my market garden plan." "This is what we've worked out with the fruit and veg.," she said, jabbing at the plan. "We can put some canes in ready for the runner beans here, the flowers can grow here. We can earmark this space for fruit trees and the other bits that are coming shortly. All in all, I think your mum will be very pleased." Then she added, without showing any sign of sarcasm,

"She a very lucky lady, having you as a son, Horace. And I'm sure she knows it and tells you often."

"I'll make sure she tells me when she comes back later on. Sam's supposed to be looking after us but he's gone out with his girlfriend but we can manage 'cos we're scouts, well nearly, but I am eleven and Olivia's a cub," said Horace innocently.

As the rotavators moved up and down in line the allotment workers took on a patch of earth each with their forks and broke up the soil so that it loosened up and became much finer. The few individuals that had been sweeping the pavement then started appearing with barrows of manure. "Mr Cox has just dumped a pile of well-rotted horse, er, kangaroo manure on your front lawn," Vera informed Horace. "So now we will barrow that all up and spread it over the tilled soil where it can overwinter."

Horace and Olivia stood on the patio surveying the scene. They were both amazed at how well everyone was working together. It was, without doubt, an exceptional team effort. Olivia took Horace's hand and gave it a squeeze. "Oh, Horace, you are sooo clever!" she exclaimed. "Mummy's going to be well pleased with knobs on with what we've done!"

"'I've' done, Olivia," said Horace, anxious to ensure that Olivia was under no misunderstanding as to who would be the (only) one taking the credit when their parents returned.

Once the allotments holders had finished their work the Horrise back lawn had been transformed. As all stood back on the path and patio admiring their work, Horace could not help but think how not only had the allotment men done what he had asked, they had done so much more. The ground had been very well turned over by the rotavators, broken up and raked smooth with a thick finish of horse manure spread over. He was very, very pleased with such a professional result.

"Before you add the finishing touches and tidy up, would you like some cake?" Horace asked the group. "I have some very nice fruit cake. We had some this morning..."

"That's very kind of you," said Vera, "and we will. But we could also do with something refreshing to drink. Do you have any tea?"

"We do, I think, yes," Horace replied. However he was a little uncertain how to make tea, especially for such a large number of people. There was no way that he was going to tell Vera this, that at eleven years old he didn't know how to make tea. Where was Olivia when he needed her? Once again he had to think fast.

"Yes, of course we have tea, but mummy thought that you could do with something that's a bit, um..."

"Stronger?" suggested one of the men helpfully.

Horace wasn't sure how something that one drank could be described as "strong." He was, after all, only going to say, "...something that's a bit more alcoholic," but in order to ensure that he wasn't saying something that didn't make sense, he just started again.

"Mummy has put some Champagne in the fridge for you to drink if you would prefer. And we have loads of Champagne glasses," Horace added helpfully. The men nodded animatedly in agreement that Champagne was far more preferable to a cup of tea. Before long most of the bottles had been opened and the men were sitting on the patio drinking their way through a case of Bollinger Special Cuvée Brut Nv. Horace had been shown by one of the men how to open a bottle of Champagne without spilling a drop. However he had also been shown how to fire a Champagne cork up in the air and catch it in a flute. With eleven attempts Horace had only broken two glasses.

With the last bottle out of the fridge one of the men suggested to Horace that he, "Shake it up a bit this time so that you can pretend you're on the winners' podium at a Grand Prix." Horace wasn't too sure what to expect, having already been told not to shake the bottles and to open them carefully with one hand on the base. Horace gave the bottle a gentle shake. "More, more," cried some of the men who then began to snigger like little children.

"That's enough, probably more than enough, now undo it like you've been shown," said one of the men.

Horace pulled off the silver foil that was wrapped around the top of the bottle, then untwisted the wire cage. He did not have time to prepare himself however - to steady the bottle and hold it slightly away from himself before easing the cork out. With a loud "pop!" the cork flew out of the bottle, missed Horace's head by a few millimetres and shot over a couple of back garden fences. The Champagne was not going to stay in the bottle either. Horace did not need to put his thumb partially over the mouth and shake; half of the Champagne came out by itself, turned to fizz and ended up down Horace's shirt. "Cheers!" said the men in unison and all of them laughed heartily as they raised their empty glasses.

"Now then everyone," said Vera. "Whilst I get the glasses washed can you chaps and ladies start to erect the bamboo canes for the broad beans and put in some posts for the fruit trees?"

"Sure thing, Vera!"

After another half hour of activity Mrs Ives appeared. No one was answering the front door so she had wandered round the back where she found what she thought was a set for The Good Life in preparation. Spotting Horace sitting on a bench on the patio with an empty Champagne flute in his hand she asked him if he had been celebrating.

"Not yet, Mrs Ives," he assured her. "I was just thinking that you could make a cup and ball game with these flutes. Look, I've tied a piece of string around this stone and I've tied the other end around the stem. Watch." Horace showed Mrs

Ives his handiwork. "You then let the stone dangle and then you swing the glass like this so that the stone goes up in the air then you have to catch it like this. Yes! Spot on! Whoops." Horace looked at the top of the flute that had broken into several pieces and fallen to the ground. "Oh, well," he said disconsolately, "that's only three glasses broken."

Mrs Ives brought Horace back to the reason for her being in his back garden. "Horace, I have six roosters in a big box in my car, which I'm donating to you. You can have them. They can live in a corner of your allotment here."

"Do they live outside?" asked Horace.

"In a way, yes, but we cage them up otherwise the fox would get them all. Mr Cox at the stables has made a lovely coop and run for them and has brought it down on his trailer. It just needs to be sited then we can introduce the roosters to their new home. They will need some pellets and corn and a water feeder all of which I've also brought along as well as some bedding. If some of the men could go round the front and help Mr Cox?"

As the coop and run were being positioned Mr Jones appeared. He staggered up the side path carrying a wooden hive. "Hallo Horace. We can't introduce any bees to it just at the moment," he explained, "but we can site it and get it ready for next year."

With all the frenetic activity that had been taking place, six o'clock came round very quickly and it was time to leave. The men packed up their tools and took one last look at their handiwork. "It's fantastic, Vera," said Horace. "The turf has gone – all to good homes, the ground's been dug, the kangaroo manure scattered, the bean poles and the stakes in place and ready, the bee hive positioned and the chickens very happy. Before long we're going to have loads of lovely eggs. I forgot to ask Mrs Ives when they start laying but I can find her up at your allotments when I need to."

"It was a pleasure to be of help," said Vera beaming, "after all that your Ravings did for us the other day. I hope your mother loves our handiwork."

"I'm sure she will, I'm sure she really will," said Horace. "She's going to really, truly love it. I'ld do anything to make my mummy happy and I think that I've definitely pulled something special off today."

"Well, we'd best be off now Horace as it's just starting to rain. It will be good for the garden though as it means that the nutrients in the manure will start to seep into the ground."

Vera walked back down the side path as Horace ran indoors. It was actually starting to rain quite heavily.

The allotment people had not long left when Sam returned home. As he opened the front door and walked indoors Horace noted that he was doing something that Horace couldn't remember him ever having done before. He was whistling, even though he was soaking wet.

"Have you had a good time, Sam?" asked Olivia, who had spent a substantial part of the afternoon watching what was going on through Horace's periscope in the conservatory, even though she could have just looked out of the window.

"I've had a great time, thank you Olivia. But you mustn't tell mum and dad where I've been or even that I've been out without you. I appreciate that it's been a bit boring stuck at home all day with not much to do but if they ask, just say that I've been doing with you what you've been doing without me." There was a slight pause and then curiosity got the better of him and he asked, "What have you been doing? Anything?"

Olivia opened her mouth to speak but Horace beat her to it.

"We've been engaged in transformational gardening," said Horace. "At least that's what Vera told us it was."

"Vera? Who on earth is Vera?" asked Sam quizzically. "Her name is familiar but I don't know why."

"Vera? She's that nice lady from the allotments. She's been round today."

"Who said you could have someone round?" asked Sam crossly, concerned that his absence would have been noted by an adult.

"You didn't say I couldn't. Anyway, you couldn't tell me that she couldn't 'cos you weren't here."

"How old is she?"

"I don't know, but she's definitely an adult 'cos she can make tea. She made tea when I was round at the allotments the other day."

"What were you doing round the allotments?"

"Helping. That's what scouts do - most of them. And now she's helped me. Us. Mummy and daddy."

"Does mum know?"

"Of course not. It's a surprise."

"I don't think mum should have a surprise. She'll be home soon and I'll tell her."

"And I'll tell her where you've been," said Olivia.

"You don't know where I've been."

"I know you haven't been where you should've been which is here looking after me and Horace."

"Oh for goodness sake, Olivia. You're getting as bad as you brother."

"Well, if you must know Sam," said Olivia warming to her theme, "it's not just Vera who's been round, it's Ray and all their friends and Mrs Ives and Mr Jones."

"Look," said Sam, changing his tune. "I don't know who all these people are and actually I don't care. I'll get dinner ready for you quickly before mum and dad get home. What have you eaten today?"

"Fruit cake and Champagne," said Olivia.

"Yeah, ha, ha. Blimey, you really are as bad as your brother," said Sam mockingly, "although he has been up to something; he smells like he's been rolling around in a beer barrel."

Horace was going to show his older brother the fruits of the day's labours but he wanted it to be a surprise in the morning for him also, once it was light, so decided against it. In the meantime Sam cooked fish fingers, beans, peas and potatoes followed by more ice cream. It was well received by Horace and Olivia, so much so that they even offered to wash up.

By the time that their parents had returned home Olivia was in bed. Sam had fallen asleep on her bed whilst saying "good night" to her and Horace was fast asleep on the sofa. It was decided that he was probably comfortable where he was so was left there with his duvet brought to him rather than the other, more usual, way round. It was only ten o'clock when their parents returned home but having had a relaxing and enjoyable time they decided to go for an early night. "We have a busy day tomorrow, darling, so we need plenty of sleep," warned Horace's mother to her husband as they climbed into bed.

"Why, what's going on?" Horace's father gently demanded.

"I'm not going to tell you. But I'm sure it will be something that you'll remember for years to come." And with a little snigger she tucked herself deep into the duvet and soon they were both fast asleep, blissfully unaware of how her prediction was going to come terrifyingly true.

***

Sunday was normally a very quiet day in the Horrise household. Breakfast usually took place around lunchtime, lunch was normally missing, dinner took place at teatime and tea took place at various times in between. However, despite an almost Zenlike calm descending on the Horrise residence late on Saturday evening, it was not going to last very long into Sunday morning.

It was around half past six when the fun started. Horace's mother had partially woken up to the sound of...well, she was not too sure what it was. Or was she asleep? It was still too early to properly wake up, that she knew, and she covered her head with her pillow. But she could still hear the noise and she was puzzled. Surely no one in their road had cockerels? Would Susie have cockerels? Definitely not! Would she? They did sound very close. She began to doze fitfully.

Horace was still in the sitting room having fallen asleep after the exertions of Saturday without making it to his bedroom. His mother had closed the curtains and George had spent the whole night on the sofa with Horace, purring gently to himself whenever Horace stirred. Horace had been having a very strange dream. He had found himself in Australia where some people on a range had approached him to build a large pen for a patrol of kangaroos. For some reason there were going to be some chickens in with the kangaroos. Horace was hard at work nailing the frame together. Bang, bang, bang. Even when he had stopped nailing with a huge hammer the noise continued.

Horace woke with a start. Someone was knocking on a door. He sat up and rubbed his eyes. He realised that he wasn't in his usual surroundings and quickly and confusedly tried to ascertain where exactly he was when he saw the television in the corner of the room. He kneeled on the sofa and drew back the curtains just enough to make a small gap. There were two men at the front door. It was fairly light outside and he turned back into the room where he could just about make out the clock above the television. It was exactly seven o'clock. He looked out of the window again at the men who had by now spotted him and were waving. Parked outside in the road was a large lorry with

CHISLEHURST MARQUEES
GIVING YOU AS MUCH EXTRA SPACE
AS YOU NEED

written on the side.

Horace was puzzled. He shut his eyes and opened them again. He blinked. He looked at the men again. They were now beckoning him to open the front door. He stood up and walked out into the hallway. "I won't be a second," he said wearily and climbed the stairs. He tapped gently on his parents' bedroom door.

"Come in," a sleepy voice invited. Horace opened the door and peered into the darkness. "Who is it?" his mother asked.

"It's Horace, mummy. Mummy, there are two men at the door with a marquis," whispered Horace.

"That's unusual darling," said his mother, "and not entirely unwelcome. But I would imagine you mean 'marquee'. Don't wake your father. Just tell the men to go round the back. They know what to do. They were round during the week doing a recce."

Horace went back downstairs and opened the door to the men. There was an older one and a much younger one and they had BILLY and WEBBO respectively emblazoned across the fronts of their t-shirts. Despite the fact that it was quite chilly and a blast of cool air had entered the house, Billy and Webbo were fleeceless and jacketless.

"Morning fella," said Billy cheerfully. But before Horace could even respond with a polite "Good morning," Webbo announced, "'Cor mate, you smell worse than a llama's bum!" Horace was a little put out by this comment, not least of all because not only had he no idea what a llama's bum smelt like but also because he wondered how on earth Webbo would know. Horace just ignored the comment. Despite the name on the side of their lorry they definitely weren't from Chislehurst; Mottingham maybe, Horace concluded, but not Chislehurst.

"We're 'ere to put up Mammoth," said Billy.

"What 'Mammoth?'"

"'Mammoth' is our biggest marquee."

"Why d'you suppose we want a big marquee round here?" asked Horace suspiciously.

"Can't tell yer mate. Don't worry, we can do it without yer."

"Oh, okay," said Horace. "Mummy said to take it round the back and you'll know what to do. I'll come round and meet you on the patio."

When the three met up again by the back door Horace found that, once more, he was beaten to the opening words by the pair. "Blimey, fella. When we came round the other day to measure up we 'ad all lawn. Now we've got what looks like a ploughed up blinkin' field," said Billy, scratching his head. Horace looked out over the garden with dismay. There had been so much rain the previous evening and overnight that the earth had turned to mud and had started to pong. The mud had splashed over the path at the side and the patio was covered in small clods of earth from the workers' boots from where they had been standing the day before. In one corner of the garden the chickens were quietly watching the visitors - until one threw back its head and launched into "Cock-a-doodle-doo! Cock-a-doodle-doo!"

"Hot diggety dog!" exclaimed Webbo. "He's a noisy s*d! I'm surprised you haven't had one of the old colonels round here levelling a Beretta 68 at yer feathered fella!"

"Where are you supposed to be putting the marquee?" asked Horace, ignoring the comments of his new found friends, both human and poultry.

"Where the mud is," said Billy, all the while wondering how he was going to erect the structure without getting completely swamped in mud. "It's a nine by eighteen metre. We're goin' to swing 'er round the top part of the, um, garden and leave the bottom bit where the birds are outside."

"What she want it for, Billy?" asked Webbo, still staring at the ground.

"I don't know," said Horace. "Why does she want a marquee?" he thought. Billy tried to help.

"The missus said she wanted it for a pa..." Then Billy remembered the last words that Horace's mother had said to him just the other day.

"If anyone asks what it's for, please don't tell them. I don't want anyone to know until absolutely the last second."

"Sworn to secrecy, mate. Sworn to secrecy. Come on Webbo. Let's get started. Is the missus definitely in boy?"

"Yes. And my name is Horace," Horace said, looking rather affronted. "Sunshine" he could deal with, "young man" was fine, "fella" and "mate" a bit too familiar but "boy" although accurate, wasn't at all acceptable. He had never been called "boy" before. "If you're referring to mummy then she's in bed and she said that you would know what to do."

"Ha, ha. He knows what to do alright!" said Webbo and they both cackled.

"Okay, Horace," said Billy when they realised that Webbo's last remark had made absolutely no impact on their junior customer. "You pop inside an' make four cups of Rosie and we'll crack on."

"Yes, alright," said Horace, although he found he was suddenly speaking to himself as the men had already disappeared back down the side of the house.

Horace returned indoors feeling more than a little concerned. To the outsider looking in the preoccupation would be entirely focussed on what was about to happen in the back garden, but to a young boy who has just been asked, if not told, to "make four cups of Rosie," the concern was elsewhere. He couldn't even offer them a glass of Champagne instead. First of all he needed a dictionary.

Horace tiptoed upstairs and into his bedroom where he found a "Concise Oxford" nestling on his bookshelf. He took it down and opened it in the middle. The pages were pristine white and still had that smell of newly printed paper, even though the dictionary was in fact several years old. He thumbed his way to the Rs and then his heart sank as he read, "Rosie Lee: Cockney rhyming slang - Tea." Horace dropped the dictionary onto his bed and went in search of his brother. He walked across the landing and slowly opened Sam's bedroom door. "Sam," he hissed through the crack, "I need your help - now!"

"What is it, what do you want, what time is it?" asked a sleepy voice from somewhere in the gloom.

"It's really important. It's eleven o'clock. Please come down to the kitchen – quickly and quietly."

Horace went into the kitchen and waited. After no more than a minute he filled up the kettle with water and turned it on. That much was certain. Then he decided that something to eat would help so he cut the last piece of fruit cake into quarters and put it on two plates. The slices did look rather large but Horace imagined that they would take the workmen's thoughts off the quality of the tea. At this point Sam appeared, bent over, shuffling and yawning, staring at the ground, and asked what the matter was. "I need you to make, or show me how to make, four cups of tea."

"Oh yeah, sure. That's a nice thing to do for mum and dad. But why are they still in bed at eleven o'clock?" Sam glanced up at the clock and then at Horace. "Especially when it's actually only quarter past seven. And why are you giving them cake for breakfast and are you meant to be giving them THAT cake?"

"It's not for mum and dad. It's for the men outside. They've come to put up a marquee. And I know what the time is. Sorry. I just needed you up. They asked for tea and I can't do it."

"Alright, don't panic. Put some warm water in the teapot and swish it round. You want about four teaspoonfuls of tea in the teapot, add four mugfuls of water. When it boils stir it and leave for a few minutes then pour into the mugs and add a bit of milk and a dozen teaspoonfuls of sugar. Got it 'cos I need a pee?"

Sam shuffled off as Horace thought through the instructions just imparted. He found some teabags and gently tore them open, measured four teaspoonfuls and put them in the pot, followed by the boiling water. Just as he had added the milk to the mugs, poured out the tea and put in the sugar, Sam returned, relieved and erect. He stared straight out of the window and exclaimed, "Heavens to Betsy, what the heck in the name of catfish is going on out there? They're meant to be putting up a marquee, not turning the garden into the good life!"

"I don't know. Mummy just said that the men knew what to do." Horace decided that rather than try to have a somewhat obtuse conversation with his brother he would take the tea and cake outside to the men that would greet him this time with smiles and pats on the back. Instead he was met with instant ingratitude.

"Cake? Look Billy, cake. We've got cake for breakfast! We'ld have bin 'appier with a good fry-up, eh Billy?! Still it's better than we 'ad at one 'ouse. There was a kid there as well an' we asked for a full English and we got an egg and a lump of belly pork. Said it was thick bacon. You kids don't know 'ow to cook these day, eh Billy?!" Billy wasn't replying - he was already putting the finishing touches to the marquee frame. All that was left to do was put the cover over the top, raise up the frame and add the sides. Sam watched from the back door wincing as Billy, Webbo and their two helpers trudged all over the garden, backwards and forwards, side to side making the ground muddier and muddier and muddier.

"Tea's up!" cried Billy finally. The men appeared from inside the marquee and stepped up onto the patio bringing with them even more of the cloying mud.

"Anybody for cake?!" asked Webbo. Despite his earlier comment, all four men took a piece and judged it "Not bad, lad." However, the same could not be said of the tea. Webbo was first to take a slurp which he immediately spat out with a loud, "Bluuuurgh!"

"What the blech is that?" he asked Horace with a scowl, who by then had retreated to the back door as Sam disappeared inside.

"My brother told me how to make it," Horace said, without even bothering to answer Webbo's question.

"It's like milky sangria, but without the booze," said Billy, sipping his a little more cautiously. "It's not too bad though, but it's a bit sweet. Why's it so sweet, lad?"

"I gave you a dozen sugars each, like my brother said," Horace replied defensively.

"We 'ate sugar in tea," said Billy. "But even without the sugar it's sort of fruity. Go an' get the packet."

Horace disappeared indoors and told Sam who was hovering in the kitchen that the men thought that the tea was fruity and that it wasn't his fault. Horace retrieved the box from the cupboard and showed Sam. "Look, 'tea'. That's what it says."

"That's not all that it says, Horace," said Sam dispassionately. "It also has 'camomile and spiced apple with cinnamon'. You've given the marquee muscle men a camomile infusion with apple flavour and cinnamon fruit and herbal tea. No wonder they spat it out."

"I was only doing what you told me to."

"Look," said Sam, reaching inside the cupboard and bringing out another box. "That's what you want, 'Tetley Original'. That's proper tea. Now, start again. I'll put the kettle on."

As Sam filled the kettle once more, Horace started to carefully tear four tea bags apart. "Now what are you doing?" asked Sam incredulously.

"You told me to add four teaspoonfuls."

"You don't have to tear the little bags open with that sort of tea, you plonker. It's like pre-packed for lazy people and mum. You just put them straight in the pot. You could even, if you wanted, just put one in each mug."

"So what does it matter?"

"Well, unless you use a tea strainer your new mates are going to get a mouthful of camomile infusion with apple flavour and cinnamon fruit and herbal tea leaves in a second. And," said Sam, looking out of the back door as Webbo dispatched another mouthful of tea (and leaf) over the patio, "I think one of them has arrived at that point."

By the time that the men had been given their second - and proper - cup of tea, the marquee erection was nearly complete. "We've just got to do a few guys to stop it blowing away and then we'll be off. Tell the missus we've tried to keep as much of the mud off as possible but it ain't bin easy."

Five minutes later and they were indeed off. No sooner had Chislehurst Marquees turned their lorry around and driven back down the road than there was another knock at the door. Once again Horace was the only Horrise family member around to open it. This time it was Ray from the churchyard, looking neater than neat. Gone were the shabby clothes from the other Saturday. Instead he was dressed in jacket and tie with a little metal fish in his lapel.

"Hi, Ray," said Horace. "Anything the matter?"

"No, not at all. It's just that your mother rang the parish office to enquire as to whether she could borrow some tables and chairs for a pa... Whoops. Nearly said it! Silly me! Sworn to secrecy you see! But I bet there'll be cake! I presume the, er, event is taking place on the front lawn given that your mother has turned the back garden into an allotment?"

"Er, yes, I suppose so Ray, but I wish I knew what you were talking about. How many has she asked for?"

"We have fifteen tables and a hundred chairs." Horace looked puzzled.

"'One hundred'! Don't you need them for your church service thing or don't you have those anymore and just do the gardening?"

"Yes, we do normally have church services on a Sunday Horace, and we use the chairs when we have coffee afterwards in the church hall. But your mother has made a very generous donation so the vicar's going to tell the congregation that they'll have to stand today."

"What about the people that can't stand? After all, anyone who goes to church has to be quite old and would have to sit down, wouldn't they?"

"Yes, the older members would, and they can just sit on the floor. However, we do have a few younger ones also and they're bringing the chairs."

"Where are they then?"

"The tables are just coming. We've put them on the stables' trailer. We could hardly carry them all down the road from the church. Here they come now," said Ray, as he began to wander back down to the road to look up to the corner as the tractor with fifteen clattering tables came round and down then parked outside number five.

"So where are the chairs?" Horace called out.

"The younger members are carrying them down, two each. They'll be here in a second."

The tractor driver jumped down and he and Ray carried the tables onto the front lawn, opened out the legs and positioned them in five neat rows of three on the grass. By the time that they had finished, Ray was smeared with straw and bits of manure. "Never mind," he said to Horace looking at his open mouth before Horace could produce any noise, "I smell a bit like you now!"

Horace was lost for words, but Ray wasn't. "Here come the chairs!" he said as around fifty young people came marching into sight and onto the front lawn, then started to tuck the chairs neatly under the tables, "Six to a table and leave ten for spare." But Horace wasn't looking at the table and chair configuration, he was looking at all the young people. Many were older than him, but not old old. "Maybe Ray's hired them in like mummy has with the tables and chairs," he thought. As the last chair carrier came into view, Horace did a double take. It was Archie – patrol leader and Raving!

"Hallo Archie," said Horace who then added without waiting for a return greeting, "Do you go to church?"

"Yes, I do now. It's just as well you've got a big front garden isn't it?" Horace ignored his question. Horace was the one asking the questions.

"Do all these children and young people go to the church?"

"Yes," said Archie, who knew that most of them did.

"I thought that church was full of old people," said Horace who by then realised that a few more faces were familiar, but not as familiar as Archie's.

"It is, but they are not the only ones. After all, they were young once. People just don't get to fifty and say to themselves, 'Oh, I'm old now so I can go to church'. Well, some might if they like biscuits." Horace had difficulty taking so much in so quickly, especially as he was in the middle of the preparation for a big event although he had no idea what the event was.

"So, did you already know Ray?"

"Not really, and he doesn't know me, obviously 'cos I'm too low down. But I know that he's a churchwarden."

"A 'what?'"

"A 'churchwarden.'"

"What's that then? What does he do?"

"I think it's like a prison warden. He has lots of keys and knows everyone, doesn't smile often and can arrest people. That's all I know." Horace thought for a bit before responding.

"I don't think church sounds too much like fun if you get locked up. What else do you do?"

"We play football and talk and eat pizza."

"That bit sounds like scouts."

"It is a little. But we don't get a uniform or badges and we don't do hikes or camps or fires. But it's still quite good fun. You should come along sometime."

"Maybe, but I can't today. Something's going on and I haven't a clue what. So once you've finished with church do you think you could get the Ravings down here for eleven o'clock? I've got a feeling they may be needed."

The young people left almost as quickly as they had arrived. Horace wondered for a short while whether or not he was in a dream but decided that it was unlikely although he wasn't one hundred per cent sure. "After all," he thought, "if I'm having a dream I wouldn't know I was so how do I know that I'm not at the moment?" He went back indoors and climbed the stairs. "Mummy," he hissed through his parent's bedroom door. He heard sounds of movement so waited for the door to open. Shortly his mother appeared at the bedroom door in her dressing gown and, without enquiring as to Horace's well-being after his night on the sofa, asked if the marquee men had left.

"Yes, they've put a marquee up in the back garden. And jillions of people from the church came and put up loads of tables and chairs in the front garden and how do I know that I'm not dreaming?"

"Stuff your dreaming, Horace. The front garden!" his mother exclaimed. "Why the front garden? Why on earth would they put the tables and chairs in the front garden? I go away for one night..."

"You were here when Ray arrived mummy but..."

It was too late. Horace's mother had run down the stairs and opened the front door. Horace thought of all the possible upstairs hiding places that might have to be pressed into service within the next few seconds but for now he was rooted to the spot.

"Oh for goodness sake!" his mother cried from the front doorstep. "Why couldn't they have taken them round the back? Why didn't you tell them to take them round the back, Horace? Horace?" From inside the laundry basket on the landing Horace called out,

"I didn't know mummy. Perhaps you didn't pay them enough?"

"Pay them enough? Pay them enough?! I paid them loads! They were the only place that had any chairs and tables spare! Wait there Horace." This was music to Horace's ears. He wasn't going anywhere. He couldn't easily go anywhere. It was quite comfortable where he was thank you very much, if a little smelly. The fact of the matter was he was stuck. His mother walked through the house to the back door and peered outside before returning to the hallway in order to address anyone and everyone.

"Not only have the church people stuck the tables and chairs on the front lawn and in such a formation as to resemble a Harvest lunch but also I don't know why the marquee people have dumped the marquee so close to the house when I asked them to put it at the back of the lawn. It's like walking outside the back door and into a whitewashed wall! Apart from the fact that it's filthy! It's covered in mud! It may be okay for a scout camp but it's not okay for a pa... The idea was that people would be able to have drinks on the lawn by the patio and then..."

"What 'people' mummy?" inquired Horace, who could only just about hear what his mother was saying.

"Oh, just people, darling. Look, Sam must move all the chairs and tables - just leave one out the front for the

Champagne - into the marquee and you can jet wash the patio. It's covered in mud. The marquee people have made such a mess. I can't believe it! I simply can't believe it!"

"Mummy, we don't have a jet wash."

"WELL USE THE HOSE THEN! Where's the peach schnapps? I need to ice the cake." Sam, who had not gone back to bed but who had retired as far as the sitting room, was lying on the sofa listening to his mother. "Peach schnapps in the icing? That's original."

Horace's mother was just about to open the freezer door when there was an almighty great screech from upstairs. She put down her tumbler of schnapps and ran upstairs to find Olivia screaming. She was as white as a sheet. "What on earth's the matter, darling?" she asked, crouching down and taking her daughter in her arms.

"It's the...the...the...laundry basket! It's moving and it's making moany noises! Oh mummy! It's haunted!" Horace's mother calmed Olivia down and then gingerly lifted off the lid and peered inside.

"And what are you doing in there young man?" she asked.

"Meow," said George as he jumped out and ran down the stairs.

Horace's mother went back down into the kitchen to locate the cake tins from their hidey-hole. Horace, meanwhile, had crept downstairs and out of the front door and round the back without even putting his shoes on. He unravelled the hose, set the nozzle to full and started to shift the mud off the patio and onto the edge of the marquee.

"Horace Horrise!"

"Horace Horrise!"

Horace turned round to see his mother standing at the back door looking less than pleased. "Come - in - here - at - once!"

"Yes, mummy."

Horace put down the hose and went back indoors. His mother was sitting at the kitchen table. Three cake tins were on the table with their lids removed. "Horace. Where are the fruit cakes? Please don't tell me you've eaten the fruit cakes."

"No mummy, I haven't eaten the fruit cakes." In the short time that Horace had before answering her question, so as to reassure her that he was not making anything up, he had decided that he hadn't eaten all the fruit cakes, just part of one, and that that didn't constitute "fruit cakes."

"Well, where have they gone? Sam hasn't eaten them and Olivia won't have done." Horace realised that there were limited truthful alternative answers to the one that he had previously given. The best option was to blame those that were already in trouble. Better that a few were in big trouble than many in a little trouble, Horace rationalised.

"It was the marquee men, mummy. They wanted a cup of tea and something to eat." It was of no consequence to Horace that Billy and his team had eaten less of the cake than he had, it was merely that if they were going to get a

Horrise rocket in due course then if they were going to get a Black Arrow they might as well get a Falcon nine point one.

"How on earth did they find them?" his mother demanded. "I hid them."

"They were looking for a screwdriver, mummy."

"In the saucepan cupboard?" His mother was incredulous.

"They didn't know that it was the saucepan cupboard until they looked and then they found that it was the cake cupboard as well."

"Well why didn't you stop them?"

"I did sort of. I stopped them from eating all of the cake."

"How? How did you manage that?" It was time for Horace to come clean, or at least slightly cleaner.

"By eating some myself, mummy."

"But why?"

"'Cos you tell us people shouldn't eat alone so I joined them and..." but Horace's mother had heard enough.

"I knew it, I knew it! They've given us a muddy marquee, they've put it in the wrong place and now they've eaten daddy's... they've eaten nearly three fruit cakes! How many were there of them, Horace?"

"Four, mummy."

"Four! That's three quarters of a fruit cake each less a bit for you. There's more fruit in one slice than someone's five-a-day. That'll teach them alright! They'll probably be on the toilet for a week!"

"Mummy, someone keeps ringing the doorbell." Horace could have gone and answered it but he thought that the distraction would calm his mother down.

"It'll be the caterers, darling," said his mother, not giving him the chance to decide whether to answer the door himself or not. Tell them to take the food and drink round the back to the marquee and set up as they wish on some tables. Hopefully Sam's moved a few, if not you can help him. And TAKE OFF YOUR SOCKS!" she cried as Horace stomped muddy footprints through the hallway. He opened the door to three young and one not quite so young women all similarly dressed with white blouses, black skirts and pink waistcoats. Three were not much older than Sam, the fourth was probably their mother. She had a name badge with "Viv" on it.

"Hi," said Viv. "My name's Viv. You can call me 'Viv', but the girls call me 'Mrs Mum'. We're from Chislehurst Catering. We've come to set up for the pa... er, for lunch. Where do you want us, round the back?"

Horace pointed the way to them then ran back through the house to the back door avoiding his footprints and in doing so adding a new set which meant that there was now a continuous brown streak along the length of the hallway. He pulled off his socks in the kitchen and started to put on his wellingtons when his mother asked him where he was going. "The marquee."

"In your wellies?" she questioned.

"Er, yes. Well I can't really go in my socks and wellies are quicker to get on than my shoes."

Outside Horace found the four woman standing on the path, each holding a couple of large containers. They were staring into the marquee through an open partition not saying a word. Horace broke the silence.

"Everything okay?" he asked politely.

"Er, not really," said Viv, not taking her eyes off what befell them when they entered, if they dared.

Sensing their unease Horace said, "Don't worry, it's only a bit of mud." Then he decided to up the anti a little. "Weren't you ever scouts? 'Cos if you were you wouldn't let a bit of mud worry you."

"Come on girls," said Viv taking a deep breath. "We can do this. After all, the guests are going to be in the same mess."

"What guests?" asked Horace.

"No idea," said Viv as she took her first steps into the mud bath. For mud bath was what it was fast becoming. It had stopped raining a while ago but why was it still so muddy? The ground was covered over by the marquee. "Don't put anything over there," said Viv pointing at the house end. "It looks particularly muddy in that area."

Horace walked round to investigate and found that he had absentmindedly left the hose on. So although he had completely cleared the patio of mud, he had in doing so helped move several kilos of mud into the marquee with the addition of a considerable amount of water.

Just as Horace was wondering what he could do with this particularly wet patch even more visitors arrived. A man and three women appeared beside the patio. The man coughed politely and Horace walked over to greet him. This group didn't look for one moment as if they were going to say, "We can do this." The man was smartly dressed in a dinner jacket with winged collar and bow tie. The three women wore long hair that nearly reached the bottom of their shimmering evening dresses. "Can I help you?" asked Horace politely.

The man cleared his throat. "I am certain that you can, young man. I and my entourage are Chislehurst String Quartet. We have been booked to play at David Horrise's pa... er, at a function in the marquee from twelve noon until three post meridian. Could you show us the way to our stage so that we may settle, prepare and conduct some breathing exercises?"

"Yes, of course," said Horace with an ostentatious bow and a swoop of his hand. "This way." Horace led them to the side of the marquee and from the safety of the path he pointed inside. "Over there in the corner will be the best place."

Chislehurst String Quartet looked across the mud via Viv and her team who already had mud up to their ankles and, by a quick examination, appeared to have no feet. "We can't possibly play here," said the man with no more than a moment's thought. "We have been booked to play in salubrious suburban surroundings in Chislehurst, not an Old Elthamian's mud bath."

"Oh, come on," said Viv who had been listening to the exchange. "We're here and we're doing the food. All you have are a few squeaky old instruments! So why don't you just put up or shut up?"

Mr Chislehurst String Quartet was not impressed. His cheeks reddened and he looked as though he was going to explode. Instead, he turned to no one in particular and said, "'A few squeaky old instruments?!' I have never been so insulted in all my life! Come on ladies." And on that final command he turned on his heels and marched back down the side of the house followed by his entourage and was never, ever, seen again at number five.

Horace wandered back indoors and found his parents and siblings in the kitchen eating breakfast. As he took off his wellingtons his father announced, "Horace, you stink. I'm not sure what you stink of but it is something fairly familiar and not very nice. Go and get washed and changed but..." he held up the palm of his hand as Horace tried to slip past, "...not before mummy has said something."

"Yes, thank you darling. Now then everyone, as you will no doubt remember, it's daddy's birthday today. This year it's what we adults call a 'landmark' birthday and because of this I have put on a little surprise celebration. We have a marquee and the caterers have just arrived. At twelve noon around one hundred guests will arrive. There will be friends and relatives old and new. We will serve them Champagne on the front lawn as they arrive and Horace you can see to that - with a friend or two if you like. The Champagne's in the wet fridge and the glasses are in those boxes over there by the door. The guests will then progress to the marquee where Viv and her friends will serve lunch. Music will be supplied by the Chislehurst String Quartet. They will be arriving shortly. Then there will be a few..." Horace's mother stopped mid-sentence and looked at her younger son. "Horace, is everything alright?"

At this point it was Horace's turn to go as white as a sheet. "Horace, what is it? What is the matter?"

"Nothing, mummy. I just need to go and get changed. I need to be prepared."

Horace climbed the stairs, his brain working overtime on a day when it should have been having a rest. Some things his mother knew about, others she did not, but was just about to find out. He needed a plan and quick. It was almost eleven o'clock and he had to be sure that he had everything worked out in the next few minutes and certainly before the guests started to arrive. It was just his mother that was going to be a bit of a problem for the time being. He would sneak out and hide in the bougainvillea until the Ravings arrived. He also needed pencil and paper.

***

Noon arrived quicker than Horace felt it should have but his mother was more than ready for her guests. She was showered and dressed. She just had to make sure everything was in place that could be in place – cake or no cake. She was going to make sure that today would be the best day of her husband's life, apart from their wedding day of course. Nothing was going to spoil it. First she went to the front door and looked outside. There was one table with ice buckets, Champagne flutes with napkins underneath but no Champagne. "Maybe it's still in the fridge?" she thought and went into the kitchen to check. She opened the wet fridge door and then shouted "HORACE!" louder than she had ever shouted his name before. Horace leant over the banister rail dressed in only his underpants.

"Yes, mummy?" he replied, quieter than he had ever whispered to his mother before.

"Horace, come down here at once!"

"I can't mummy, I'm getting washed and dressed - as daddy told me to," as if that justification would seal the excuse.

"Horace, have you drunk the Champagne?"

"No, mummy." Horace thought that had his mother asked, "Do you know where the Champagne is?" or "Do you know who drank the Champagne?" his answer might not have been so straightforward. But she hadn't so it was.

Horace's mother, with the cake incident still fresh in her mind then asked, "Have you drunk any of the Champagne?"

"No, mummy."

"I don't understand. We only went away for one night and one day, hardly twenty-four hours. SAM! OLIVIA!"

Horace's mother didn't have time to go and find her other children for cross-examination because at that precise moment the telephone rang in the hallway beside where she was standing. She took a deep breath, composed herself and picked up the 'phone. "Hallo, Karen speaking."

"Good morning, Mrs Horrise. This is Edgar Fripp from Chislehurst String Quartet. You will recall how we have spoken at length recently about our booking, how you wished, nay required," (Mr Fripp nearly spelt out each letter of 'required' as he spoke it) "us to dress, what we were required to play, what time we would arrive, how long we would play for, the particulars of our refreshments bearing in mind our preferences and intolerances, where we would sit..."

"To be honest, Mr Fripp, and for the benefit of accuracy, those were actually your requirements. I am more interested at this particular moment in WHERE ARE YOU?"

"I was coming to that, Mrs Horrise, if you would just listen for a moment and please don't raise your voice as it affects my ears' perfect pitch. Chislehurst String Quarter arrived at your abode a short while ago to prepare by setting ourselves up and executing a few breathing exercises. I was met by a ruffian who directed us to a muddy marquee with an even muddier ground which resembled a child's giant mud bath, not the raised decking that we are used to so that our music and our manner can fl-hote over the heads of the guests, thus providing them all with a multi-sensory experience. When I suggested to the ruffian that we would need something a little more in keeping with our attire as well as our status and standing in the community, a young woman in an outfit that would have been more in keeping with what one would expect to find in a t-hart's boudoir than an exclusive semi-suburban gathering remarked, without solicitation, that all we had were 'squeaky old instruments' despite the fact that my violin is a replica limited edition Messiah Stradivari Violin of 1716, and that we should 'put up or shut up'. So we shut up, even though I had only uttered one sentence, and left. I am now at home having my hands waxed with a Lomi Lomi massage to come. Goodbye."

Horace's mother carefully put down the 'phone and sighed - a deep sigh, a very deep sigh. Her cake had been eaten, the Champagne was missing, the musicians had left without playing a note, the marquee was unbelievably muddy and for some reason the lawn had disappeared. She slipped on her shoes and tottered out of the back door. Immediately she bumped into Viv who was carrying more food trays into the marquee. "Goodness me, Viv, what has happened to your shoes?!" Horace's mother had looked down at her feet and found that they, along with the last twelve inches of her legs, were caked in mud and from her waist down to her knees fair splattered.

"To be honest, Karen, I thought that the mud was all part of the experience. I thought maybe we were going to be entertained with a mud fighting competition later."

"Most certainly not! But what's all this talk of mud? Mr Fripp's just rung me to complain." Horace's mother followed Viv to the marquee entrance and there she stopped. From the safety of the garden path she looked inside at the chairs and tables that Sam had expertly arranged, a corner space with no musicians, catering more or less ready, but where was her lawn? She blinked – once – twice, then opened her mouth and then closed it again. Had someone laid a mud carpet for some sort of joke? She was unable to speak. She turned on her heels and considered that maybe she was at that particular moment suspended in a dream but she wasn't. What was it that Horace had asked earlier, "How do I know that I'm not dreaming?" The answer was that you just know! It was real, too real, far too real to be a dream. Now what? Once back in the kitchen she called Horace, "HOR-ACE!!!" But there was no reply, just a handwritten note on the kitchen table, written in pencil. It read:

"Dear mummy

I thought you wanted your garden doing. I'm sorry that I've got it all wrong. I don't do it on purpose. I want to be a best son but I seem to be the worst. Your lawn is some at Susie's, some at the memorial garden and some at the allotments. I don't know how I'm going to get it back.

Horace x

PS. I was only trying to do my best."

Horace's mother put the note down and then put herself down. She sat down heavily on a chair. She crossed her arms on the table, rested her head on them and closed her eyes. No cake, no Champagne, no musicians and no lawn. Just mud, mud, not glorious mud, a bee hive, some plant paraphernalia and a load of noisy cockerels. It was all a complete disaster and the guests had not yet even started to arrive. But when they did they would scowl and comment and criticise and leave and social media and who could blame them? "Thank goodness I'm not on Trip Advisor" she thought.

"Is everything okay, darling?" Horace's mother looked up and greeted her husband with a pathetic little smile through her tear-stained face. He was dressed for the mixed lounge at the local Chesney Golf Club with "smart casual wear." She thought he looked impeccable and as handsome as the day that they had first met, if not more so, but all she could say to him was,

"Darling, do you think you could take me out for a short drive?"

"On the golf course?" he asked brightly.

"No, darling," she said despairingly, "in the car."

There was no one at the front of the house as they jumped into the A6 and drove a short distance to Watts Lane. Horace's father parked, the couple alighted and sat on the bench with its stunning view over the Kyd Brook valley and beyond. There was silence for several minutes then Horace's mother spoke, "Happy birthday, darling."

"Thank you Karen. Please don't be too upset; we still have each other." This was a cue for the pent-up angst of the last few months, brought to a head that very morning, to surface.

"But it's because I have you that I wanted today to be perfect. I've been planning it for months but all I have to show for it is an effing marquee that looks like it's come back from a 3rd Chislehurst winter camp and a bunch of caterers who think they're working on a farm in the middle of the monsoon season in South Asia."

"Come on," he said, putting his arm gently around her shoulder. "let's get back and face the music; some of the guests will have started to arrive."

They drove slowly and disconsolately back to the house. However, as they pulled up in front of the drive their countenance rapidly changed. They couldn't quite believe what they were seeing. Most of the guests appeared to have already arrived and were engaged in animated conversation on the packed front lawn. But what was it that they were drinking? Horace and the rest of the Ravings were busy pouring out glasses of what looked like Kir Royale, a drink comprising burgundy-coloured crème de cassis topped with Champagne. "My goodness, darling," said Horace's father, "it looks like the boys and girls have got their hands on some Champagne after all."

"The only fly in that particular ointment is that the cassis isn't being served out of a cassis bottle and the Champagne isn't in a Champagne bottle. It appears to be pre-mix and it's coming out of demijohns and through a funnel," said his wife critically. But she didn't say it too loudly and certainly wasn't going to complain too much. Any sudden and unexpected elation was hanging by a thread and there was no way that she was going to be responsible for its breaking.

Horace's parents alighted and cautiously joined their guests at the edge of the throng. "Sorry we're a bit late for David's own birthday, but we had to go and get some fresh air," announced Horace's mother to no one in particular. However, despite this admission of lateness she sensed that she was not actually getting anyone's attention. She looked around at all the smiling, happy faces and, listening to so much laughing and giggling, had the feeling, although she knew otherwise, that she was coming in at the end of a party not the start of one. Someone pressed a glass of burgundy something into her hand. She took one sip and was jolted back into the present as she pronounced, "Good golly by the grace of goodness! What on earth is that?"

"Not Kir Royale that's for sure," said her husband who was standing nearby. She didn't have to wait long for an answer.

One of her husband's oldest friends sidled up to them and said,

"This sloe gin is so magnificent! So strong! So well-bodied! Apparently the sloes have been steeped for over a year! And they're British! So much better than boring old Champagne! A master-stroke, David. A master-stroke. Matured with age. You and it. Excellent! Well done!"

"Yes, yes, indeed, thank you and you must thank Karen. She organised it all." However Karen had gone off in search of a Raving to interrogate them as to the source of this successful aperitif. She grabbed Archie, who was the nearest to hand.

"Horace said he felt responsible for the Champagne that went missing so he got hold of some of Bert's Sloe Gin, six large glass jars' worth to be precise."

"Who's 'Bert?'"

"He's a new friend of Horace's sort of, He makes his own sloe gin and we have six gallons of it which is just as well 'cos it's going down like there's no tomorrow."

"Six gallons?" thought Horace's mother. "That's half a bottle each!"

It was at this point, just as she was wondering what else lay in store for her, which was somewhat ironic given that it was her husband who was supposed to be having the surprises, that Horace appeared on the front lawn, stood up on a chair and hollered, "Lunch is served in the marquee round the back! Don't forget the footwear code!"

Now it was Horace's mother's turn to go as white as a sheet as she started to shake. "They can't have lunch in the marquee! They can't have lunch in the marquee!" Sensing her disquiet Charlie came ambling over and asked solicitously,

"Is everything okay, Mrs Horrise?"

"No, it's not!" she squealed, "The marquee is hiding quicksand!"

"All taken care of, Mrs Horrise. Follow me!" Charlie held out his hand and led Horace's mother down the side of the house where Melanie was dispensing four black bags to each guest.

"As we announced as you arrived, double bag each foot then tie with the handle bits round your knees. You can't go any further until you've been checked by Olivia and Emily." Horace's mother looked distraught at the thought of her husband's guests having to don temporary wellingtons in order to have lunch but as she regarded the smiling faces as they tried, some fairly unsuccessfully, to step into four bags then tie them up, then walk, she thought maybe it wasn't too bad after all. Great Uncle Stanley, who wasn't the tallest person on the planet, had lost the plot completely. He had stepped into two bags and tied them together round his trouser belt then put the other two on his arms and tied them together round his front and back. He was so nearly completely covered in black bags that he resembled some sort of bondaged geriatric punk from the 1970s.

Once past quality control, Viv was offering canapés followed by Edward leading guests to a table, squelch, squelch, squelch. As soon as everyone was seated tables